SCAR

A DARK MILITARY ROMANCE

LOKI RENARD

Cover Design: *Eris Adderly*

Photographer: *Paul Henry Serres*

Model: *Jonathan L-Laurin*

For more of this sort of thing, please visit:

www.badgirlbooks.com

❀ Created with Vellum

1

KEN

The first line of defense is a receptionist. Blonde. Pretty. Vacant behind the eyes.

"Get out of here. Go home."

Her smile wavers. Her hand moves toward the phone.

"No. Seriously. Get your bag. Go home."

She looks at me, her soft civilian brain struggling to comprehend what's happening. A tall man in a nice suit is telling her to leave her place of work in the middle of the morning and go home. She knows she should stay, but her hand is already reaching for her purse.

She's conditioned to stay at work until 5 pm, but she's also programmed with a deeper instinct, and that's to avoid angering unknown males in their prime. We're all animals. I'm more animal than most.

"Good girl."

She gives me a nervous smile as she leaves the building. She's probably as complicit as the rest of them, but I don't like killing women if I don't have to.

They don't have security on the lower floors. Security down here would imply that there's something to guard. The resistance will come once I get up the first set of stairs.

She is up there. Waiting for me.

The moment they gave me her details, I folded her picture and put it in the pocket closest to my heart. I'm going to get her back from these monsters if it kills me.

I walk through the lobby and into the hospital proper. Down here it feels like a nice place, the perfect spot to come if you want to do a bit of plastic surgery tourism.

"*Guten morgen*," a blond man greets me from a desk inside the door. I can see other staff moving around the place. They're all blonde. If not by genetics, by bleach.

"Hi. I'm here for Mary Brown."

He frowns ever so slightly and taps the name into the computer. "I'm not sure we have a patient by that name, sir."

They do a good job of keeping up the facade. Nose and boob jobs on the lower floors, torture on the top. All neatly compartmentalized. These fuckers know precisely what they're doing, and they know how to hide it in plain sight. Their sick ancestors were never brought to justice, and somehow that twisted entitlement has filtered through to this generation. It's all I can do to stay calm as he looks at me with those flat blue eyes.

"I'm sure you don't. I'm sure she's a serial number to you. Or a barcode. The technology has changed over the past few years, hasn't it?"

No expression passes over his passive plastic face. "Sir, I'm afraid we do not have a Mary Brown. What is your name, sir?"

I walk past him, down the hall. I know there will be an elevator coming up on my right, and next to it, a set of stairs.

"Sir?"

I reach the elevator, and push the door to the stairwell open, taking the steps three at a time. My source says they keep the projects on the top floor. There's ten floors to the building. I race upstairs, moving faster than the elevator can.

I'm sure they've already sounded the alarm, but there's not much they can do. Their security is lacking because they're brazen enough to believe that there are no consequences. They've turned this part of South America into their own little personal Eden, bribed all the necessary officials, bought all the souls they needed to buy, and almost nobody knows or cares what goes on here.

Until now.

The door to the tenth floor opens directly into a ward of sorts. There are rows and rows of beds, perfectly starched white curtains hanging between them to make little cubicles. The floors are clean. The walls are pristine. Everything here is perfectly orderly and at a first glance, if this were just a picture in a book, you would think it was a perfectly normal high-end hospital room. You wouldn't know it was hell on earth.

Standing here, despite the silence, I can feel the suffering. There are dozens of people in here. Every bed is occupied. Not a single one of the occupants stirs as I walk past. They are awake, but still.

I walk slowly down the corridor between the beds, feeling the slow, burning anger in me rising with every step. Fire and brimstone have nothing on this silent ward with its white walls and bleach scented floor. This is where the world ends. This is where the semblance of any kind of human passion fades away.

I've seen death before. I know the face of war. I would rather listen to shells whistle over my head and sink rounds into the enemy than stand here where not a single one of these people can fight back.

I wish I was here with a team of choppers. I wish I could evacuate them all. But I can only save her. I've got to find her. Now.

The 'patients' are equal in number and gender. Males on the left, females on the right. I walk down the right-hand row, looking into the pale, calm faces of the people who lie there. Most of their eyes don't move toward me. I don't know if they're sedated, or if they're just absent. The human mind will flee when it has endured enough.

Many of them have fluids going into them and out

of them. Needles. Bags. Tubes. Blood. Urine. Bile. All contained in pristine plastic.

My fists clench by my sides. There's not a one of them that isn't in dire need of rescue, but I am one man and I have come for one woman.

When I lay eyes on her, I don't recognize her at first. She's pale. Her dark eyes are so much wider and larger than they are in the picture that came with her profile. There are two scars, one running beneath each of her eyes. Those are the ones I can see. I am sure there are others running the length of her body. That is what they do here. Cut the living. Cause them pain. This is a laboratory for pure suffering. This is where calculations are made to determine what a person can take. How they can be harmed and yet still remain alive.

The silence is telling. These are people who have learned that screams only feed their tormentors. These are people who have withdrawn so deeply into themselves that they do not feel the world outside their minds.

Cold anger has been brewing inside me. It bursts into full fury as I look at this girl whose eyes see me and yet do not react.

"Mary?" I say her name softly. "I'm Ken. I'm taking you out of here."

She stares at me. Through me. She doesn't even blink. Has she heard me? I don't know if she's even capable of hearing me anymore. How much have they damaged her?

The door at the far end of the room opens. Heavy feet land on the floor. These people stamp when they walk, heel first like ducks. She flinches. It's the tiniest reaction, so small that I'd barely notice it under normal circumstances. Right now, it's as heart wrenching as if she'd screamed out loud.

She is so small. So helpless.

I turn around, put my body between her and the people who are coming. How many times has she needed me before this? How many times has she cried out for help that wouldn't, couldn't come?

As their steps draw closer, I grit my teeth and I smile. It's not a pleasant smile. It's a grin of pure feral fury. I'm not afraid of being caught. I could have come into this place secretly. I could have avoided the potential for violence and their attempt at counter capture. I chose not to for a reason. They're going to pay for what they've done. They're going to pay a thousand times over.

"Hands up, *bitteschon*."

I turn to see five men. Two armed guards and what look like three doctors. Two of them hold needles and the others hold guns likely loaded with ammunition more dangerous than bullets - tranquilizer which will turn me into one of their subjects.

These sick fuckers are so arrogant even now. They see me as a potential captive, because they live in a world where they dominate absolutely everything and everyone. The notion of someone being a threat to them doesn't even occur.

6

I can't afford to give them the chance to lift the barrel of their guns. Violence explodes. My body becomes a chassis of death hurtling across the small space they have foolishly put themselves in with me.

I have a dozen weapons at my disposal. I choose the knife. Thirteen inches of folded tempered steel makes short work of these men who are used to victims too sedated to move and too frightened to fight back.

Bones snap. Blood flowers on the pristine white floors and walls, arterial spatters and shrieks of horror. Their victims don't scream, but they do. They scream perfectly, outrage and pain and the rattle of death.

None of the bodies in the beds nearby move as the monsters are slain. I wipe my knife off on one of their all too white coats and return it to the sheath underneath my coat.

It was over too quickly to be truly satisfying. I'm almost disappointed, but I have a feeling I'll kill again before this is over.

MARY

Someone cries out for help in the distance. In the fog of my despair I sense motion nearby. A pair of feet flies by upside down at the end of my bed. Beautiful crimson is painted across the walls. It has been so long since I have seen color. I feel my dry lips curl with delight at the sight.

"Mary?"

The first time he looked at me I thought he was one

of the frequent figments of imagination which have plagued me almost as long as I've been captive, but for a second time the man enters my field of vision. It takes some effort to focus my mind. My thoughts have become increasingly fractured as the days pass by, one day very much like the next except for the fact that every time I wake there's a little less of me. I am shrinking into nothing in this bed.

His eyes are a slate gray, but the left one is half tinted with green. They're the strangest eyes I've ever seen, and they're set in a face which is pure masculinity. Hard jaw, low cheekbones. Thin slash of a mouth set below a rugged nose.

"Can you hear me, Mary?"

I nod. The motion feels strange. Nobody has spoken to me directly in months.

A knife cuts the bonds holding me. They fall away as if they were never there at all. He helps me to stand, takes one second to note how wobbly I am on feet which haven't been used in weeks. He shakes his head and grabs my arm, lowering his shoulder. With a practiced move, he chucks me up and over his back and pulls me snug up around his shoulders, wearing me like a cape.

I wonder how he got here, how he got past all the doctors and all the scientists. Then I see how. They're littered around the place like discarded trash. They're dead, purposefully, definitely, utterly dead.

Months ago a sight like this would have made me scream. Now it makes me angry - not because they're

8

dead, but because those deaths came too easily. This man is clearly a professional. He killed like one. Too cleanly. They should have suffered longer, harder, felt more pain.

He carries me into the stairwell and down the stairs. I hold on tightly to him, my arms wrapped around his neck like a child's, my head spinning.

Round and round and down and down we go. Is this really happening? I can feel him, but even the motion of his muscular body supporting mine isn't enough to convince me that this isn't a vivid hallucination. I squeeze him tight, lean in and breathe to smell his sweat. My tongue creeps out a fraction so I can taste him too. Male sweat and exertion, slightly salty, a hint of musk. He tastes incredible.

My greatest fear is that I might wake up, as I have so many times before, still in that bed, still unable to move, still at the mercy of the descendants of monsters.

He cranes his neck to look at me. He's wondering if I really just licked him. In that moment of perplexed connection, I know this is real. No hallucination wonders if you're going to take a bite out of them.

We leave the building. Step out into the sun. I feel wind. I feel heat. I feel the world rush back around me, color and sensation, wind and heat assaulting my senses. It is a gorgeous cacophony which I can barely make sense of. I close my eyes against the light and huddle into him. I have been absent for so long, and now I am riding with my head propped on the shoulder of a beast of a man who came from nowhere.

How is he doing this? Nobody stops him. Do they know of the dead lying upstairs? Wide eyes follow us, but nobody questions him. I catch a glimpse of him in a reflective surface and see his expression. His face is a mask of death in potentia. Nobody wants to ask the reaper why he carries a woman from this facility.

There's a car waiting outside. He puts me into the back of it, shuts and locks the door, gets into the driver's seat, and we leave. That's how simple escape is. For now.

KEN

She lies limply in the seat where I stowed her. I'm not entirely sure she's conscious, or if she knows what's going on. Her slim frame is clad in the long white scrubs, and I can't see what condition she's in. As soon as we stop, I'll have to inspect her thoroughly. They didn't have any tubes going into or out of her, not like some of their bedridden patients who were basically pale plastic porcupines, but that doesn't mean she's okay.

Her first words to me are ones laced with revenge.

"Thank you for killing them."

"You're welcome."

I glance into the rear view mirror, both to look at her and at the traffic behind us. You can't walk into a Schutzenarbeit Laboratory, take a subject and ride off into the sunset. Pure brazen arrogance just worked, but it won't work again, and they won't let her go easily.

They've put work into this girl. They're going to want her back.

Sure enough, within ten minutes SUVs emerge from the flow of traffic. Heavy vehicles. They're scrambling a response. Late, but they're coming. They love the color white, so the vehicles stand out like sore thumbs.

I don't have the backup I need out here. This girl isn't high value enough to attract a dozen man unit. Her family can't afford to pay more than one man, and the truth is, they can barely afford to pay me.

We're going to have to fall back to my secondary position. I turn the car off the main road and head down a side street. They likely think I just walked in this morning, but I've been here for a month, setting up my options and my escapes.

As we speed past a corner, an old woman pushes a barrow full of melons across the road. The melons go flying as the car behind us smashes through them, sending red flesh soaring into the sky.

I met with her yesterday, knowing I'd need an escape route and several distractions if things went wrong. She has five hundred American dollars tucked away somewhere, more than enough to replace the melons.

It's slowed them down just enough to allow me to skid around a left hand corner and put the car into a garage. Five people come running to pull metal gates shut behind us, and 0.2 seconds later, the convoy comes rushing past outside.

We're safe. For now. But we have to move.

The people who just helped us get away will get to keep the car. I take my supply pack out of the passenger seat, sling it on my back, then go around the car and pull Mary out. She's pale and I don't know how aware she is of what's going on. Hopefully not too much. This is a shit show.

It's one thing to get the girl out of the hospital. It's something completely different to get her out of the country in one piece. They'll kill us both before they let the evidence of their experimental program get loose.

"I'm going to pick you up again," I say, warning her. I don't want to startle her. And I want her to know she's safe with me, that she's been rescued, not just snatched away.

She mumbles softly. I slide my arms beneath her back and knees and pull her out of the car. The locals have prepared a room for us, but it's a bit of a walk to get to it. We head down a flight of stairs which open from a hatch in the floor, and I carry her through a dark underground passage - a smuggler's tunnel.

Crime is rife in this part of the world, but heroin dealers are nothing compared to the people we just escaped from. The shaft leads underneath several city blocks, and is remarkably well developed, with ventilation running up through tiny passages and cracks to little spaces in various houses, along with chutes for dropping packages. This city is a place of snakes and ladders, and fortunately, plenty of hiding places for people who need to escape.

US dollars go a long way here, so I've been able to set aside my own little piece of subterranean heaven for us. A flimsy wooden wall with a padlocked door awaits us. The lock matches one of several keys I have on a ring. Each one of them is specific to this operation.

I juggle Mary and the lock, then swing the door open and carry her into the little shanty. It's not as bad as I expected it to be. They really rolled out the red carpet for us down here. There's a toilet with a small partition, and a bench with a sink attached. We've got water. I'm actually impressed.

There's even a little bed, an old mattress covered with a blanket that looks maybe halfway new. I settle her down on the bed, and start the little stove in the corner.

She lies quietly on the bed, so quietly I lean over and take her pulse. It's steady, but it's not the strongest. She could go into shock now and die, just from pure fucking relief at being rescued. Sometimes, people wait until they're safe to pass away.

It's somewhat similar to dealing with a starving person. Giving them one big meal can be fatal. You have to re-feed them just a little at a time. Get their bodies used to processing nutrition again.

She needs to take things slowly. She needs to be kept quiet. She needs time to recuperate - but we really don't have much in the way of quiet or time at our disposal. We can stop a few hours at most, but we're going to need to get moving soon.

"Mary?"

Her eyes flutter open. I can see some of the wounds they've inflicted on her body, but there are even more of them on her soul, written in her eyes. She flinches and looks around.

"Where am I?"

"Somewhere safe." It's a lie, but a lie she needs to hear. We're still in the heart of their territory and if they find us... even the thought makes me grit my teeth. I've been radioing for backup, calling in favors, but it takes time to get people into the area - and an influx of special ops mercenaries is something they're going to be looking for now.

She's weak. The micro-tremors in her fingers worry me. She's lost weight in captivity. I'd put her at about a hundred pounds tops, too small for a woman her height. She needs nutrition and she needs it regularly.

"Drink this."

It's a protein powder in water. It tastes like a sweaty jock strap left in the back of a locker and fermented for a few months, but it's good stuff and she needs it.

She doesn't even grimace as it touches her tongue, so I know she's been starving.

"Good girl," I murmur as she drains it to the very last drop.

"I'm not a good girl," she replies, her voice weak. I almost see a speck of mischief in her eyes, and for a brief moment I can imagine this young woman as she would be in her prime. Full of life, and full of trouble, no doubt.

"How did you end up in there, Mary?"

She shakes her head and shrugs. "Bad luck."

I had hoped she would be more forthcoming than the contact who funneled this assignment to my unit. Mercenary life is full of questions. So is the military, really. I've spent my adult life following orders, rescuing people I'm told to rescue, killing others I've been told to kill. It would be nice to know why I just murdered ten German-speaking scientists in a facility that technically doesn't exist.

"You can tell me."

"No, I can't," she says. Her eyes catch mine. "You know I can't."

I could make her tell me. Easily. But I'm not going to. She's been through enough.

"They were experimenting on you," I say, probing a little more.

"Yeah."

"Why? Something special about you?"

She shakes her head. "It's what they do."

"What are they trying to learn?"

"Everything."

She's being vague, but specific enough for me to fill in the blanks. These people are the kind to be curious for curiosity's sake. They're the grown up versions of the kids who pulled wings off flies. Except now the flies are human, and now their techniques are far more refined.

"Did they do serious harm to you?"

She turns her eyes away from mine and closes her mouth. My question wasn't specific enough. Of course they did serious harm.

"Do you need treatment? Want to see a doctor?"

"Fuck no." She shakes her head. "I'll die before I see another doctor in this lifetime."

"Alpha Protector, do you read me?"

A voice comes over my comms. Thank god.

"Reading you loud and clear," I respond.

"Helicopter is two clicks out. Have her ready for transport. We're getting in and getting out."

"Who is that?" Her eyes flick toward the sound.

"That, my dear, is the cavalry."

Mission accomplished.

2

KEN

Thirteen months, three weeks, two days. That's how long it's been since I laid eyes on Mary Brown. No. That's not her real name. I never found out her real name, even though I looked into it for a good while. She was in my care for less than an hour, but I couldn't get her out of my mind. I looked for her afterward. Never found a thing. She disappeared like a damn ghost.

And now, in a military mess in the middle of Afghanistan, I found her. I come back from a mission and see her just sitting there casually, as if she's been in my life all along. At first, I can't even believe it's her.

Her glossy dark hair is tied back in a ponytail. Her eyes are somewhat sheltered behind a pair of dark-rimmed, rectangle shaped spectacles. She wears basically a flight-suit, a camo tan outfit that's just snug enough to show the curves of her hip and her ass.

She should sink into the background. She's certainly trying to. Soldiers are milling around her, relaxing, drinking, carrying on. She's sitting stock-still on a hard metal bench in front of a table, working on a laptop with a gaze of intense concentration. Her fingers work over the keyboard at a frenetic pace, and I can tell she's not really aware of her surroundings at all. I'd disapprove usually, but it makes me smile because it tells me something that warms my heart: she feels safe.

I stroll over, slide my way onto the bench on the other side of the table and wait for her to glance up at me. Her eyes never leave the screen. I guess I'm going to have to get her attention another way.

MARY

"Hello, young lady."

That voice slices through time, hits my nervous system like a drug. My thoughts halt. My fingers stop. I freeze like a rabbit, and for a few seconds - far too long, I do nothing at all.

Lifting my head is the hardest thing, but I do. And I see those eyes. The face of the man I thought I'd never see again. The only man on Earth who knows my secrets. My pain. The only man to ever see my scars. He's sitting in front of me, broad shouldered and faintly smiling.

"Hello." I force the word out as my heart starts to race in my chest. We're a million miles away from where he found me, but his presence brings it all rushing back.

He is the reason I'm alive. I never had a chance to thank him. I have a sudden impulse to throw myself into his arms, but I refrain. There's a table in the way anyway.

"Come and talk to me," he says, rising from the bench. He's so goddamn handsome. I wasn't in the right frame of mind to appreciate his physical attributes when we last met. Now its different. My gaze roams over the expanse of his chest, his tall, muscled physique, the way he holds himself erect. Underneath that shirt, I'm sure his torso is as hard as his face. And oh my god what a face he has. That jaw. Those cheekbones. All hard and rugged and exposed to the elements. There's very little soft about him. He's built for pure action - and not just any action. There are athletes who are attractive, but not in the way he is. He is built to bring death.

Everything about Ken is extraordinary. The five o'clock shadow on his jaw, those bicolor eyes which are calm, but can be so damn fierce, the rugged brows and hair just long enough to be tousled with sweat and dirt. He's been out in the field. There are a few faint smears of what I'm sure is blood on his shirt and pants. Someone else might not notice it, but I know what he looks like covered in the sanguine secretions of his enemies. I remember everything. I remember him.

I follow him to a corner between two shipping containers outside the mess, not exactly secluded, but a little more private. I don't want people overhearing what he has to say anymore than he wants to say it in front of others.

"So, what are you doing here?" He quirks a brow at me as if I've done something wrong. "I would have thought you'd have had your fill of excitement."

"Have you?"

"Have I what?"

I've confused him. I guess I have to explain. "You're running around in war zones, so why wouldn't I be doing the same?" I lift my chin a little, defying him to bring up what he knows. I've worked too hard for too long to leave that horror behind me. I've thrown myself into my work, and I'm not going to let one nightmare stop me from ever sleeping again.

I guess he expected me to run back stateside and cower for the rest of my life. Hell no. What I went through won't define me. Not ever. And I won't let him define me by it.

"I didn't go through what you went through," he says.

"You didn't," I agree. "*I* went through it. I decide how much it affects my life. Not you. And I decide who knows, not you."

Both brows go up. "So you're telling me that you haven't disclosed your... prior experiences to command here."

"No. I haven't. And I haven't disclosed the boo boo I

got on my knee when I was six either," I say, pushing the limits of sarcasm. "It's nobody's business but mine."

He opens his mouth, but before he can piss me off more, someone even more obnoxious interrupts us.

"Good, you've found each other," a man with the swagger of a commanding officer strolls by, claps him on the shoulder and points at me.

"She's going to be embedded with you."

"We're not doing the kind of work suitable for journalists," he says, instantly trying to get rid of me. I don't blame him. There hasn't been a single officer in this country who has wanted me as a tag along. Afghanistan is no place for people who can't pull their weight, and embeds aren't allowed to.

"Nobody here is doing work suitable for journalists," the guy says. I should know his name, but I've already mentally dubbed him *General Douchebag* and I can't store endless names for every asshole I meet along the way.

I have press credentials, and I have a right to be here. The same right the rest of them have. Not that General Douchebag cares about that. There's only one way to earn a man like that's respect, and I fucked that up long ago by being born without a penis.

"Take her out, send her back when she shits her pants," Douchebag says. He walks off without so much as a word to me. Rude. I try not to give a fuck about rude. I'm out here for the stories they don't want me to get. Of course, the thing about stories that people don't want you to get, is that they try to stop you from getting them.

There are a lot of ways for officers to obstruct journalists. First, they usually try to bore you, drive you around until you get tired of dirt and sand. I've been on the Afghanistan equivalent of a tea cup ride for many weeks. Then, if that doesn't work, they try to scare you. I don't scare easily, so that hasn't worked. Now we're entering phase three: put you somewhere you might actually die and kind of sort of hope you do. Most people tend to get out at that point. Not me.

There's no need for the military to be paranoid about embedded journalists. The number of people who care about war journalism has dwindled since Vietnam. Most people don't care about the situation on the ground in Afghanistan, or Kazakstan. Any of the stans, for that matter. They hang around on social media, waiting for a meme to tell them what they should be outraged at that week. A disinterested populace with a ten second attention span is not exactly a lucrative market for journalistic rigor. Most of what I do ends up back in military hands, in their publications and journals. A lot of it never sees the light of day. Maybe one day I'll write a book about all this. Make it fiction.

If I do, fictional me will be sexier. She won't sweat as much as I do. She won't always wear long sleeves and pants to hide the scars inflicted by her captors. She'll throw her head back and she'll laugh at the foibles of the world instead of steaming with fury at every insult.

She won't secretly be terrified of everything. She won't insist on putting herself into dangerous situation after dangerous situation just to feel like she's alive, because every time she tries to live a normal life she's swamped by terror that only goes away when bullets start flying. She'll do it because she's driven by things like purpose and bravery.

And she'll be respected by the men, who of course, all want to marry her. Not bang her and discard her, treat her like a notch on their belt, but who aspire to have her in their lives for as long as they both shall live.

Unfortunately, real me falls far short of fictional me. Real me is shorter, fatter, frizzier. Real me is motivated by anger that keeps the fear at bay. Real me is itching to see what goes on in the clandestine corners of this war that isn't a war, and real me doesn't really care what my personal outcome is.

I could write something based in reality, I suppose, but nobody wants to read about some barren victim being scorned by men and sometimes women who think they're better than her by merit of their service. Hell, they probably are. I might be in harm's way almost as often as them, but mine isn't a noble sacrifice. It's ignoble in the extreme, truth be told.

"I guess I'm stuck with ya," Ken says. He doesn't seem as upset by that as I thought he would be. Maybe he just likes to follow orders. Or maybe he likes me, as unlikely as that seems. I'm not used to being liked by men. I usually go out of my way not to be liked. But he's different. He's the one who saved me. He is my… what was it… oh yes… *Alpha Protector.*

"You are," I agree. "Stuck with me, I mean?"

"Where's your equipment?"

"You're looking at it."

He gives me a critical once over. "I mean where's your change of clothes, your bedding, your gear?"

"I have a pack," I say. "Don't worry, you don't need to babysit me. This isn't my first time and it won't be my last."

It's strange, because I don't know him at all, but he knows more about me than anyone else on the planet. He knows the secret I have kept hidden since they day I escaped that facility. The downside to that is the fact that when he looks at me I know he sees the broken woman in the hospital bed, and I hate that.

"When will you be moving out?"

"Tomorrow morning," he says. "0300."

I nod. It's early, but that's common in the military. Getting up before the cock crows is just how they do things. It's probably even a little on the late side for him.

"Alright then, I'll be there."

"Wait a minute." He holds his hand up, stops me before I can leave. "Before I take you anywhere, we need to talk. I mean, properly talk."

"No, we don't," I cut him off abruptly.

"How did you get credentials to get back into danger?"

So many goddamn questions. I wish he'd just shut up and accept that I'm here. "You won't believe this, but I got them off the back of a cereal packet."

KEN

She wasn't a smart ass when I met her a year ago. Then again, they'd broken her to within a hair's breath of sanity. She was hurt badly, but even then I knew she was a fighter. The question is, how much of a fighter?

Her pretty eyes are locked on me with a bold defiance that gives rise to several impulses. If she were under my direct command, I'd be doing something about her insubordination, but she's not a soldier and I can't expect her to act like one. Truth is, I'm aroused by the potential challenge she represents. I like my women feisty. But, she's not here to be my woman. She's here to follow me around into some potentially seriously shitty situations, and frankly, I don't want her anywhere near them.

"Who are you trying to prove something to?"

"What?" She feigns indignant ignorance.

"We both know you belong at home."

"Oh, do we?"

Fuck. I'm trying to get through to her, but all I'm really managing to do is insult her, which isn't the plan. I'm proud of her for being out here, I am, but I already saved her cute butt once, and I really don't want to have to do that again.

She's staring daggers at me now. "If you say a word of what you know about what happened to me…"

I snort as she threatens me. "What?"

"I'll make your life a living hell."

"Uh huh."

She's not so cute now that she's trying to intimidate me - ah what the hell am I thinking, of course she's cute. She's damn well adorable. I'd enjoy this if we were somewhere safe, where a mortar couldn't come flying through the air at any minute.

This is a war zone. And a dangerous one. And not just because of ISIS and the other big names people stateside recognize, the ones with the bold flags and the catchy acronyms and the surprising social media presence. This war has opened up a place for every brutal wannabe warlord in the region, and they're in a competition to see just who can be the most vicious. Nothing is off limits in this war. I'd accuse her of being naive, but something tells me that she's not.

Innocence is usually appealing in a woman. This one has had every bit of innocence stripped away from her but it doesn't diminish her beauty. It's easy to be brave when you're innocent. We see it all the time, rookies come in at eighteen and throw themselves into action without fear - until the first time they take a real hit and see the true face of war. Then it's not so easy.

This place breaks people. But I'm not sure it's possible to break this woman. She stayed brave in the face of death. That doesn't make her immune to it. If anything, it makes her a likely candidate. And bravery doesn't mean shit without training, which I'm sure she doesn't have.

"If I take you with me, you're going to do as I say when I say. I'm not going to argue with you. I'm not going to tolerate backtalk."

"Sure," she says. "When we're out, I'll listen."

"Not when we're out. From this second. And you'll be bunking with me."

"Why?" The look she gives me is more curious than anything.

"Because I want to keep an eye on you."

It's the truth, but it's not the whole truth. *Because I've wondered what happened to you every day since you were choppered out* would be closer, but I don't know how she'd take to that, and I don't even know if I should say it. Odds are she barely remembers me, and what she does remember, she probably doesn't want to.

She gives a shrug. "Okay."

I have a private CHU, which is basically a shipping container fitted out with the basics you need to not live like an animal. They stack rows and rows of these things together. Mine's a little more private than most, but hardly luxurious. It's going to be a little cramped with two of us in it, but aside from that we should be good.

Mission wise, we should be okay too. I'm doing reconnaissance, mostly. We're looking for some ways in, ways around. Informants. That sort of thing. The work I do can't be done without local knowledge. There's even a very remote possibility that she could help in that regard. A woman can achieve some things a man can't, even out here in the ass end of nowhere.

"Get your kit and come with me."

She does as she's told, grabs her stuff from the barracks where they put her up. She really doesn't have much. A single pack. That tells me she's capable of living light. I like that about her. Hell, I like almost everything about her, not that I can express that right now.

Mary follows me to my CHU. There's already a spare bed in there. Most of the time these hold two soldiers. It's not luxurious accommodation, not by a long way. Just a simple cot bed at right angles to another one, a toilet and shower at the end. I took the bed nearest the door, so she's got the one closest to the shower by default. The only difference between them is that mine has a pair of boots beneath the bed. All my things are stashed and stacked away as per regulations.

She sets her pack by the bed and looks at me with a *well, what now* sort of expression. It's a good unspoken question. An hour ago, I figured I'd never see her again in my life. Now she's standing in my quarters, looking healthier and happier than I could have hoped for.

I have to restrain the impulse to hug her. Something about the threatened scowl which is hanging just beyond her expression warns me that will not be appreciated. She has a *don't touch me* vibe about her which I can understand all too well.

Mary has known pain - and she expects it everywhere.

MARY

He's just... looking at me. It's hard to read his expression, but suddenly it's much harder for me to breathe and this little box that counts as shelter, sort of.

I don't know what to do with myself. Other men I just give a nasty attitude, but he's the reason I'm alive. I owe him something. Hell. I owe him my life. He's literally my hero. And we're just standing here, staring at one another in a way that's more awkward than two tweens at a dance.

"I, uh..."

"Make yourself comfortable," he says at basically the same time.

"That's going to be a challenge," I say. This is not a comfortable place. It's not meant to be, I guess. It's meant to be sufficient. And it is.

I sink down on the bed and look at him as he stands there for a second, then sits on his too. Our knees are almost touching. He clears his throat.

"I'm really glad to see you again, Mary," he says. "I, er... wondered how you were getting on."

"Fine," I say. "I mean, good even."

"Good." He nods and slides his hands over his thighs. He has long legs, and though the motion is probably just to get the sweat and sand basically everybody is coated in out here off his palms, something about it draws my attention and makes me tingle between my thighs.

"So I know how I got here. How did you get here?

Didn't get the impression you were in the military last time we met?"

"Special forces," he says.

"Green berets?"

"Different special forces," he says in a tone which strongly conveys he doesn't intend on telling me a damn thing.

"And your last name is Ares?"

That's what's written on his shirt, at least.

"Ken Ares," he says, extending a hand across the awkwardly small space. "Nice to meet you."

"Mary Brown," I reply.

"Uh huh," he raises a brow and shakes his head at me. "You expect me to believe your name is Mary Brown?"

"Well it is, so…"

"Not your birth name though, is it?"

"Not quite," I allow with a small smile. I've changed my name several times in my life for several reasons. I like Mary Brown. It's unassuming and sort of classical in a way. It doesn't come with any expectations - unlike Ares. Jesus. What a name. *If you married him, your name would be Mary Ares.* The school girl thought runs through my head, and I banish it immediately. Women like me don't get married. Especially not to men like him.

Ken is a very, very handsome man. Genetics account for about half of his appeal. You can't get that frame he has without good breeding, those long legs and broad shoulders can't be earned. But the rest of him, that's pure hard work and hard living. He's worked for his muscularity, and for each of the scars he has, one running down the length of his jaw to his neck. Is that new? I don't know.

I have strange memories of him rescuing me. Some are so clear, little snapshots in time. Others are vague. For the first time in a long time, I wasn't in imminent danger of death. The feeling I had with him has stayed with me. I conjure it up when I can't sleep at night, when the memories threaten to overwhelm me, I remember how it was to be held in his arms... I felt safe.

But I was just a job to him. A job he did very, very well, but still a job. And I'm a job now, so I can't let him see how much I feel for him. It would probably scare him away, make him hand me over to someone else.

"You hungry?"

"No, I was just in the mess, remember?"

"Right," he nods and gives me a crooked little smile. "Of course. Well, you should try to get some rest. I'll put the AC on for you. Best to sleep now. Morning comes quick here."

When we were talking outside the mess, there was that flash of dominant arrogance. It was brief and he stuffed it away, but I saw it for a second and it's made me curious. What is this man really like?

"I..." I take a breath "I need to thank you. For what you did for me. In Chile."

He inclines his head a little. "It was my job, Mary. Pleased to do it."

His job. Just like I thought. He's not interested in me. Why would he be? He's probably married to some pretty woman back in the States, with a gaggle of kids. These guys are never single, even if they pretend to be sometimes when the loneliness creeps in.

"Well, thanks," I mumble. I'm embarrassed, suddenly shy. I thought maybe it might have meant something to him, but now I see that's just crazy. A man like him, he's a perfect specimen. He deserves a perfect woman, not a broken shell of one.

"No problem." He flickers a wink at me, the double colored eye flashing beneath long dark lashes.

I smile and turn my head away. It's hard to look at him. He reminds me of everything I've tried so hard to forget, and everything I will never have.

"I'll leave you to rest."

"I'm not really tired. I'll just get some work done."

I sit back on the bed, resting my back on the wall, and pull my laptop out. I have plenty more to write, deadlines to hit. Traveling through Afghanistan has been a hell of a journey, being handed from unit to unit. I've seen more than most people would want to see, and most of what I've written so far has been redacted heavily by command, but it doesn't stop me from writing it in the first place.

"I want you in bed by nineteen hundred," he says. "You've got an hour."

"Excuse me?"

"It's eighteen hundred now, more or less, so you have an hour."

"I won't be sent to bed," I say, my temper rising. "I'll sleep when I'm tired."

His brows draw down. His jaw hardens. Military types are more controlling than most. They get used to being told when to shit, when to sleep, when to shower, and they have no qualms about telling anyone who they think ranks below them the same. I'm going to set him straight before he gets into the habit of bossing me around.

"I told you that you'd do as you were told," he says, a masculine growl in his voice.

"Well, I'm not. You can order your soldiers around because they agreed to the chain of command…"

"So did you. You would have signed up to it when you came as an embed. I can send your sweet little ass back stateside before you can close that laptop if you're not careful."

"You wouldn't dare!"

"I would. And I'd spank your butt before you went, too."

"What?" My face flushes red all the way to my ears. Did he just threaten to spank me? What the hell?

"That's ridiculous," I say, my voice hoarse. Why is my throat so damn dry all of a sudden?

"It isn't. I'm pretty sure it would be necessary in your case."

Is he teasing me? I can't tell. There's warmth in his voice and his eyes, but I don't know if that means he's joking. Something tells me he isn't.

"Listen," I say, drawing myself up as erect as I can

while sitting on a cot bed. "I don't know what you think you're playing at, but…"

"I'm not playing at a thing," he interrupts. "I'm giving you fair warning, letting you know how this is going to go."

"B… but… that's…"

I wish I wasn't blushing. I wish I didn't feel as though I was shrinking right before his eyes.

"Never been spanked, have you."

He says it like it's a fact, which it is, but I don't see the point of it. So what if I haven't been spanked? Is he trying to say I'm weak or something?

"I've had a lot worse."

"Oh I know," Ken replies. "And that's the point. You don't know what a good spanking is. You don't know what it would do for you, or what the point would be. You think I'm just threatening you with violence."

"Well, aren't you?"

"Not in the way other people have," he says, his voice gruff, and serious, but also somehow comforting. "I might spank you before bed. Give you a taste of what's waiting for you if you don't do as you're told."

"You're fucking kidding me…" I shut my laptop and stare at him. "Tell me you're joking."

He rubs his hands together and the corner of his mouth lifts in what isn't exactly a smile.

"I'm not kidding, Mary, not at all. You don't want to do as you're told, I'm going to give you a reason to. Simple."

"It's not simple at all. You can't spank me!" I truly

can't believe he's serious. He's talking about hitting me. I can't believe it. I lift my laptop up and wrap my arms around it, holding it protectively in front of my body.

KEN

She looks scared. And cute. But mostly scared. Funny how she can land in the middle of one of the most brutal war zones in the modern world and not bat an eye, but at one threat to smack her deserving bottom she suddenly finds her fear.

I'm not trying to scare her. I am trying to make an impression though. There's a whole lot of ways to get through to a hard-headed brat, but spanking is the most effective by far in my opinion. Doesn't do any long term harm, but makes a good impression physically and emotionally. Mary has been practically begging for once since we met in the mess.

A more permissive soldier might be alright with a smart mouthed embed, but I am not that guy. My life depends on being able to assess people in an instant. I need to be able to tell if I'm in the presence of a friend, or a foe. I need to know if someone can be trusted, or if they're a loose cannon. Over the years, I've developed a pretty good radar for reading people.

Mary is smart mouthed, disobedient, and planning on being a handful for sure. I'm going to get well ahead of that and make sure before she goes to bed tonight, she knows exactly where she stands with me.

Might seem like I'm coming down on her hard

ahead of time, but that's how discipline works in the military. You don't wait for a problem to manifest itself. You nail that thing down hard before it gets a chance to get started.

"Ken," she says. I like the way my name sounds coming out of her mouth, though in her case, *sir* would probably be more appropriate. "Maybe we got off on the wrong foot."

The back-peddling is in full swing now. She really doesn't want her butt whacked. All the more reason to do it. Girl like her, with a history of monsters, needs to know that what I have in mind won't be torture.

Even though she's trying to seem composed, her eyes are wide, and her face is pale. She's genuinely frightened. Maybe I should back off a little.

Extending a hand across the space between us, I pat her knee gently. "Don't worry little girl, you'll survive."

She doesn't like that one bit. Her laptop is cast to the side as she lunges forward, spitting fire.

"I am not a little girl," she practically growls. "I am a woman, and you will respect my independence."

Nope. No chance of backing down now. Besides, if I hold off on giving her what I know she damn well needs just because I know her past, I'd be doing just what she doesn't want, and treating her like she's damaged.

"You don't have any independence where I'm concerned," I inform her calmly. Her face is only inches from mine and she looks more beautiful than ever. Pale fear has given way to a heated flush on her cheeks. The other end of her will be an even brighter color soon. I'm now more determined than ever to give her a good spanking. She needs someone to take her in hand, settle her down. She's brave, but it's the kind of bravery looking for direction and a firm hand.

"You can't…" she splutters. "You can't just declare yourself my owner."

Her words make me grow hard. Owner. Yes. I want to be her owner. I want to possess her completely. I want to throw her down and ravage her tight little pussy, but right now she needs a spanking, and it's a spanking she's going to get.

"Over my knee, little girl."

"Don't you call me that," she growls.

This is devolving into an argument. I'm not going to tolerate a battle of wills. That completely defeats the purpose of this entirely, so instead of saying another word, I take her arm and give her a quick tug.

She tumbles over my lap with a little shriek of surprise, her nice full ass presented adorably in the flight suit which is tight over her hips and rear. I'd rather spank her on the bare, but I don't want to strip her naked right now. She's frightened enough as it is. Having the padding of her clothing will dull the sting a bit and ease her into the concept of discipline.

"Settle down," I soothe, snugging her close to my body, one arm wrapped around her waist.

"Let me up!"

"Not until I'm done with you. I'm not going to

spend the next month arguing with you. You're going to learn to do as you're told right now."

"Ken!"

Oh I really love the sound of her saying my name, especially gasped in that breathy way which sounds almost as excited as it does frantic. I don't know how she'll take this. It could make her even angrier. It could make her break down completely. I don't want either of those outcomes, but I can't control everything. I just need to control her.

I rub her bottom once or twice just to calm her down, then swat her. It's not hard enough to seriously hurt her, but it is more than enough to get her attention. She gives a little yelp which is just damn well adorable. I want to hear it again, so I swat her again, my hard palm finding her sweet, soft bottom.

She's perfect. I can't believe she's in my arms. Well, over my lap. There's hardly a day that's gone by since she was taken away that I haven't thought about her. This wasn't what I'd planned to do with her, but turns out she needs it and I'm more than happy to give it. This is a side of me that rarely gets free reign. It's one thing to command men and women in the field, but to dominate a spirited woman in the bedroom, that's what really excites me.

I spank her bottom again, my palm covering one cheek entirely, cupping her cheeks. I can't really feel what lies beneath the thick fabric, not entirely, but the gentle swell and roundness of her cheeks is just evident enough to make me want to see more.

This woman is driving me to distraction. My cock is rock hard, even though I know there's no chance of getting laid. This isn't foreplay. This is discipline.

"You are going to do as you're told, young lady," I lecture as I start spanking her in earnest. "You are going to listen to my orders and you are going to follow them. If you don't, you'll find yourself right back here over my thighs, having your bottom spanked."

"Ow!" She complains in return, gasps and yelps and similar sounds escaping her with every swat. I'm barely spanking her really, but she's rolling her hips and squirming against me for all she's worth, and it's enough to grind my cock into a near painful state of arousal. If I didn't know better, I'd almost think she was doing it on purpose.

I spank her a little harder, hoping to settle her, though that's a counter-intuitive thing to do and it doesn't work at all. The harder swats make her yelp and grind and… was that a moan?

I rub my hand over her wriggling cheeks and give her another firm swat nice and low. The sound she makes is definitely carnal.

"Little girl, are you listening to me?"

My hand slides from around her waist and tangles in her hair, giving me leverage to lift her head up and pull it back, the other hand sliding down over her cheeks, my fingers finding the space between her thighs. If there wasn't so much fabric down there, this would be lewd.

Her hips rise, pulling her pussy up into my hand. She wants this. She's giving herself to me. If we were anywhere other than a box in the middle of the desert, if I didn't know what she'd been through, I might give into the desire to take her the way I want to. But I'm still worried for this woman, and as tempting as it might be to take advantage of the heat between us, that's not what this moment is about.

MARY

What the hell is happening? It doesn't hurt. Not in terms of how I've come to understand pain over the years. There's heat in my ass and fire running through my veins. This is embarrassing as hell, and the last thing I expected him to do to me.

I'm shocked, but not as angry as I should be. When he first called me little girl, pure anger flashed through me. To my ears it sounded derisive and dismissive, as if I wasn't strong enough or good enough to be here with him.

Then he made me feel his strength. Then I got to feel what I always wanted, his strong arms wrapped around me - maybe not how I thought I wanted it, maybe not entirely how I do want it, but being held over his lap and talked to in those low, masculine tones triggers the needs I push away, the needs that made me so angry when he first began to encroach on them and now are starting to flower within me.

"You're going to do as you're told," he murmurs, his

palm rubbing over my heated cheeks. "You're going to get some sleep, little girl. You're going to lie down, get comfortable, and get some rest."

His voice is deep and soft and calm. There's no anger in what he's doing to me, even though I could easily accuse him of brutality and the worst kind of domination. He is dominant. I don't think he knows any other way to be. But he knows how to handle it, and me, and in spite of my stinging bottom I'm... impressed. Impressed and aroused.

With just a handful of swats, he's completely addled my brain. I've gone from wanting to scream in his face to wanting him inside me, and that's obviously out of the question. The fact that he's sliding his big hand between my legs is probably incidental. He can't be doing it on purpose. He wouldn't...

I feel his fingers drag across the very core of me. There's a lot of cloth and stuff in the way, the jumpsuit, jeans underneath, underwear under that. It's a shitload of clothing to be wearing in the desert, but it makes me feel safe. Hides the scars. I could wear less, but I'd feel people's eyes through the fabric, seeing what I don't want them to see.

His hand slides back over my bottom and lands with another heavy swat.

"You understand, brat?"

"Yes." What other answer can I give? He's got me at his mercy, balanced on the edge of pleasure and pain, panic and relaxation. I could sink into his grip and let him have his way with me, or tumble into anxiety.

Even I don't know what I'm going to do. I haven't been with a man since the laboratory had me. I planned to never be with one again. I won't show my scars. I won't let anyone see what was done to me.

His hand slides back down between my thighs, but not across my pussy. He finds the inside of my leg and holds me there by the upper thigh. I'm not sure what he's doing, but it's obvious he's not done with me, and he's not going to let me up yet.

"Why are you here, Mary?"

"What?"

"I mean why did you come to a place like this? Is this your way of self-destructing?"

I would never have had this discussion if he hadn't broken down my resistance, taken me off guard, and held me like this. I wouldn't have been able to. Some small but powerful voice in my head would have told me that I couldn't. Right now, that voice is silent. I don't know where it went, but I can speak now.

"I came here to live," I say softly. "I… I tried to go back and hide. I tried to be normal. But normal felt fake to me. It felt… hollow. I don't think it's for me anymore. I don't think it ever will be."

KEN

She can't possibly know it, but what she's describing is the precise reason I keep re-enlisting. In between stretches of service, it's also why my private work has always returned me to these parts of the world. It's common for people who have been in war to feel as if they're unable to settle into everyday life anymore. Mary was never a soldier, but what she's been through is probably equivalent in a lot of ways. Hard times make hard people, but general society doesn't have much space or time for hard people. Especially nowadays. Now it's the softer the better. Safe spaces and things. That's fine for them, but it's not for us.

A lot of people back home don't understand. They think that people like Mary and I must not feel fear. Truth is, we're just afraid of different things. Places like Afghanistan are safe havens for those of us who need danger to feel not just alive, but normal. It doesn't make sense, but it's true. Out here, things are hot, disgusting at times, depressing for some, and certainly not nice. But this sandy hell calibrates you, makes something simple like a shower seem like heaven. Everything is ultra real out here. Nobody smiles and tells you to have a nice day because they're hoping for an extra dollar on their tip, or because they've been made to by some manager. The men and women out here don't have time for any pretense besides simple military bearing. Life is difficult, but it's also easier in some ways. Eat, shit, survive.

She gets that. But I'm thinking unlike military personnel, who at least have comrades who understand the lure of war, she's probably been alone with what feels like a horrible secret and a twisted soul. I've always felt connected to her in some intangible way.

Now I feel even more for her. I'm going to guess she never got therapy for what happened to her. She has 'feelings are weakness' written all over her.

"Alright," I tell her. "Then I won't send your ass home yet."

"Gee, thanks." Her sarcasm returns full force. Only because she hasn't had a good, long, proper spanking yet. I'd love to strip her bare and paint her ass bright red. Hell, I will do that soon enough, either when she's ready, or when she doesn't give me any other choice.

"I wasn't kidding earlier, Mary. I expect total obedience from you. Most embeds spend their time shitting themselves in the back of LAVs, but I'm guessing that won't be what you do."

I can feel the smirk, even though I can't see it.

"I'm not afraid of the Taliban."

"Well you should be," I lecture her. "This is their world. They know this land like the back of their hand. This is where they grew up. They know every rock, every tree, every road. And they know exactly where to bury their bombs and lay their traps."

"And we've been here for over a decade," she snorts. "Long enough for us to know the same stuff, right?"

"It's not the same."

It really isn't. The people here are built from this land. We are foreigners in it. Hiding from a world which moved on without us and left us, we're warriors out of time and space. The people we fight are something else. I've seen the way people here blend with the territory, melt into mountains, slip into sand. We have two advantages keeping us alive: training, and technology. Take away our resources, and all we have left is our wits. Sometimes they're not enough.

There are a lot of stories that never get told in this part of the world. I hope she doesn't discover any of them.

"So, are you going to let me up?"

She asks the question with that smart ass casual tone which tells me she's already gotten a little too comfortable over my thighs. That fits with what I know about her. Put some pressure on her, make the situation more intense, and she'll relax. If I was to be gentle with her and speak to her softly, she'd probably panic. That's my suspicion anyway.

I need to know. So I lift my hand and I start stroking her bottom gently, rubbing up to her lower back. It's a nice soothing touch, designed to calm, and most people would find it relaxing. I see tension creeping into her muscles right away. She tenses up and everything feels harder than it did before. She's not soft and relaxed anymore, she's waiting for something.

"Let me up, Ken."

There's an edge to her voice that wasn't there before. I could keep stroking her, soothing her. I could let her up. Or I could do what I planned to do all along - smack her little butt nice and hard.

"Ow!" She gasps and I feel her body relax again, draping over my thighs. A smile twitches the corner of my lips. Oh yes, she's going to be fun to domesticate. And maybe, in doing it to her, I'll do it to myself.

I give her another swat to the other cheek, then let her up, trying not to smile too broadly as she scrambles to the other side of the CHU - all of three feet away.

MARY

Fuck. He disarmed me and I wasn't even armed. My face is hotter than my ass, which is still stinging.

"Don't do that again please."

"I won't if you don't deserve it," he says evenly, his handsome features so composed as he sits there, straight backed and powerful. "But I'll put money on you deserving it sooner rather than later. Ready to get cleaned up and go to bed?"

"Fine," I agree. He's won this round and I don't have the energy for another one. It's way too early to be going to bed. Even with a 3 am start time, I'm going to get more than ten hours sleep if I somehow manage to fall asleep now.

"Good girl," he says, his deep voice rumbling through me, going right to my core. God. I can't even look at him. He spanked me. He fucking spanked me. I mean, not really. It wasn't like he pulled my pants down... why the hell am I thinking like this?

"I'm going to take a shower."

———

The shower is a tiny box-like space with a shower head that has seen better days and a floor that squeaks and flexes beneath my toes as I step under a fairly futile spray of water. The notion of washing my hair under this is a struggle, but I set to work anyway because it gives me time to think.

I've been out here for months now. I've seen some stuff. Mostly I've seen the backs of military men and smelled their sweat. At night, in the bars that inevitably spring up in bases, sometimes I hear their stories. These are some of the bravest and best people I've ever met.

Ken isn't like most of these men. Something sets him apart. Something it's hard for me to put a finger on. He's... wilder somehow. When I look into his eyes, I get a feeling right in the pit of my belly. It's a similar feeling to the one I get when I visit a zoo and look at a tiger behind wire. Not quite fear, but awe.

He's an impressive specimen. There are a lot of men out here who are brave and muscle bound, but he's the only one who gives me that feeling when I look at him. Maybe that says something about him. Or maybe it just says something about me.

I don't know. I'm confused as hell. But I am glad for the privacy this little "bathroom" provides. There's literally just a shower and the toilet on the other side. Basin big enough to bathe a mouse in for washing your hands. I'm guessing they don't get used much out here.

I don't like being naked much these days. The scars could be worse, but I wish they weren't there at all. It's not that they're grotesque or dramatically disfiguring. You could mistake them for simple surgery scars, because that is what they are, thin, clean lines traversing my waist and abdomen.

Most people wouldn't know what they were. Might think they were appendix scars, or maybe c-section scars. But I know what they are, and Ken will know what they aren't, is my guess.

I've been marked forever, externally and internally. Physically and mentally. I can forget about it when I get dressed, but the minute my clothes come off, I see those marks again and I can't pretend it was all some horrible nightmare.

He can't see me naked. I won't let him.

That decided, I dry myself off as best I can and climb into the fresh clothes I brought with me. Blue long sleeved shirt and pajama pants. They're for men, really, but they're loose and they're comfortable and the collar makes them practically semi-formal.

When I get out of the shower, he's turned the AC up a bit. It's cool inside the CHU, and my bed is waiting for me, corner of the blankets turned back, my pack and boots stowed beneath. I didn't do that. He did.

He's sitting on his bed, laying ammunition out in order from biggest to smallest. The biggest is almost comically large.

"Is that a 50 cal round?"

"Uh huh. Desert Eagle," he says, pulling back a piece of fabric over a case to reveal the drab olive of the monster weapon. Basically a handgun on the prover-bial steroids.

I should know more about guns, but I mostly leave

the shooting to other people. It's not like they let embeds have weapons anyway. The rules of engagement are tight out here, and that's caused most of the problems I've encountered so far. It's not good enough to spot enemy actors. They have to have effectively engaged a unit first, which, in practice, means someone gets to be shot before the units around me can do a thing about it.

"Get into bed."

I bristle at the order, but we do have a deal and I don't want him to grab me and smack me again. Pajamas don't offer the same level of protection my clothes did earlier.

I get into bed and lay down. Neither of us say anything. He turns the main light off and puts a smaller one on next to his bed. He can't know this, but I never sleep in the dark anymore, so that little glow is perfect as I reluctantly close my eyes and attempt to go to sleep at an hour I haven't slept at since I was about four.

KEN

She's more tired than she thinks she is. We all are out here. As soon as the light dims, she's done for. After about ten minutes, her breathing starts to slow. Five minutes after that, she's fast asleep.

I feel a sense of peace I haven't felt a long time, having her here, in my room, watching over her as she gets some rest. It's as if some anxiety I didn't even know I'd been carrying around has been satisfied. Even though we're basically strangers. Even though we hardly know one another at all, she feels like she's mine.

I've got to be careful of that though. She might not feel the same way. Probably doesn't, in all likelihood. She seems to remember me, but how well. And I don't want her to succumb to me just because she feels some misplaced sense of loyalty or worse, like she owes me something.

Once I'm finished getting ready for tomorrow's work, I grab a shower and get into bed as well. 0300 comes quick.

3

KEN

We're rolling in a Frankenstein. A not so armored vehicle that's been done up by a few genius engineers who can't walk past a bit of steel without welding it to something with wheels.

Hillbilly armor, they call it. Just shit welded on wherever it'll fit. It'd be nice to have the full sleek military machines you see in movies and training videos, but in real life, the military industrial complex is held together with duct tape.

If she's afraid to be rolling around in this patchwork quilt of spare parts, she doesn't show it. I'm not sure she actually realizes what we're in. It was pretty dark and she was still half asleep when I got her out of bed and into this thing.

There are three other guys with us. This is basically reconnaissance, roll out into the depths of a Middle

Eastern night and see what's happening. They like to move at night when it's cold, and when they think we're not watching. Heat sensing technology lights them up like Christmas trees though. Right now it's a pitch black ocean of dark danger out there.

We move slow. There are bombs everywhere. It's not safe to take the tracks we usually take, and it's not safe to go off-track either because they'll put them in both places. We have a Soteria device located above the cab that scans for the things, but nothing is perfect. Basically, we're playing minesweeper.

"Fuck," the driver's buddy curses as a blip lights up on the monitor. There's a damn daisy chain of the things laid out near the ridge we're wanting to ascend. The people we're fighting aren't high tech, but they understand the basics of war which never change, like securing high ground.

It takes us a long way to pick our way through and find a safe spot to look out over. We could have done this with drones, but a drone can't do much about a problem. It can only identify it. While we sit, the others are transmitting information back to base about the mines and their location. Some of the bomb squad will come out and deal with them, hopefully successfully.

Intelligence suggests there's a weapons pipeline running through the valley below. Most of the time the local boys avoid valleys. They're too easy to set up ambushes in. But they also have shit lines of sight for most of our tech, and as many of us are out here, we can't cover everything all the time.

The war is being fought beneath our noses. We cover this country like an electronic hawk, and still they manage to get away with transporting the essentials of war: weapons and fuel.

As night turns into day, and our post becomes completely visible, we back off and head away. If they were out there, they moved earlier, or some scout spotted us and warned the others off.

Dawn is breaking as we head into what's supposed to be a friendly village. Mary is impressing me so far. She's dead quiet. She literally hasn't said a word since we started. I've nudged her a few times to see if she's awake and alright, but she's alert and quiet. A little huntress, her dark hair slicked back into a bun behind her head.

Some of the village kids come running, hoping we have something for them. There's a bag of candy we got for them. Winning hearts and minds with melted chocolate from the other side of the world. The women don't come near us. They stay back, shades of black and red and brown, covered by their hijabs. There's still a lot of suspicion and mistrust around. They're liberated today, but they're worried we'll pull back and the Taliban will sweep back in. It's not an entirely unfounded fear. We can't stay here forever, but these people will live and die within a hundred miles of where they were born. They're living like we all used to, at the mercy of war bands who rush through, kill men, carry off women, and leave everything to burn if it doesn't meet their satisfaction.

We stop in the village and get out. I have a couple of contacts I'd like to talk to, men who are brave enough to risk horrible deaths to give us information. I tell Mary to stay in the vehicle. If we have to make a quick exit, I don't want to have to rush around and find her.

MARY

I love talking to the women in villages like these. So often it is the women who suffer most in silence, and it's the women who rarely have their stories told. In this part of the world, it's common for one man to have several wives.

When Ken moves away, I get out of the LAV and see if there's anyone wanting to talk. A lot of the younger women are curious when they see an American woman, so usually it doesn't take too long for some of them to slip up to me.

I've learned enough Pashto to communicate basically, and sure enough, soon there is a small group of ladies congregated about me, fascinated by my clothing which is modest enough not to scandalize them, but so much more practical than their own in many respects. Their children cling to their legs, looking up with wide eyes. Some of the older ones giggle at my broken sentences.

I have a few supplies I like to share out, nothing special, just hotel shampoos and soaps, little treats they appreciate because most of the time they don't make their way out to rural Afghanistan, and the little money they have in their households rarely stretches to toiletries. I give each of the women a little bit of eau de toilette and some soap. They secrete it in their clothing as fast as they can. Jealous eyes make for swift stealing out here.

They tell me that it has been three months since the Taliban left, but before they did, they warned a fiery retribution for anyone who allowed the invaders in. These people are expected to resist and to fight, even though there is no chance of them being able to do that. I know that they welcome us because they have no choice. Most of them have never known anything other than a life under occupation. This part of the world has been broken so many times it feels like it might never be whole. This is where civilization began, more or less. It should be the most advanced. It should be full of gleaming cities and great works. It should be a beacon of human advancement, an example to civilizations born later. Instead it is dust and rubble, people scraping out subsistence living as they have done for thousands of years. There's probably a lesson in that somewhere, but I'll be damned if I know what it is.

Their names are Asal, Larmina, and Damsa. Asal and Larmina are sisters married to a man named Mohammad. It may be two different men, but in a rural village like this, there's a high chance it's the same man. Polygamy is the way of the world where the male population is decimated by war. Damsa is married to a man named Mustafa. The others cringed when she mentioned him, so I take it he is not popular for some reason. They are all beautiful, but their hard lives are taking an inevitable toll. Asal tells me she has had seven children, of which four still live. Larmina has two, but she is only a new bride. And Damsa has six living. They ask me where my children are. I just shake my head and their eyes grow sad. Some things are universal, the regarding of children as blessings. Out here, they truly are. Sons work fields, daughters bear more sons. It's brutally unfair in so many ways, but they know no other way. Years ago, I would have felt nothing but pity for them. Now I have a different understanding. There is not one world. There are a thousand worlds in a thousand places, maybe a million, maybe there's effectively a world for every individual on the planet. At any rate, people do what they can with what they have. They pity me and I pity them, and what is the point of that?

Halfway through our conversation, the women squawk and fall back. At first I have no idea what is frightening them, then a big shadow falls over me, and a large hand grips me by the upper arm.

"I told you to stay in the LAV," Ken growls down at me. He's trying to maintain his friendly face for the benefit of the villagers, but women of all nations and all languages know a displeased man when they see one. More than one sympathetic glance is cast in my direction as they hurry away.

"I'm ten steps from it," I argue back.

"I said inside. Not ten steps. You can be taken at ten steps," he growls under his breath. "Get in the vehicle."

Okay so he's pissed now. Fine. Whatever. I'd trade that risk for ten minutes talking to these women. Women know more than anyone gives them credit for. That's true almost everywhere, but especially here. Women hear things they're not supposed to hear. Women talk. There's no internet out here. Information travels at the speed of gossip. If he had any damn sense, he'd be asking me what the women were saying, not barking at me for doing my damn job.

I get into the LAV. The others are still outside, waiting for his orders. Apparently he's going to deal with me in the cramped confines of this mutated mini-van. I try to get to the back, put myself against a wall where he won't be able to do anything but growl at me, but as he gets in, he grabs me by the back of my head, his fist grasping the hair at the back of my neck.

"Let go of me!"

"No," he says, giving my head a tug. "You didn't listen to me. I explained it nicely before, but I guess I'm going to have to explain this much less nicely now. You don't take a goddamn breath without my permission, you understand? If you were military, I'd be wearing your ass out for the next month."

"I'm not military. I'm a journalist. And you need to let me the hell go." My words don't really make sense, but we both know what I mean.

"I don't care what you are, you're still going to goddamn well do as you're told."

"I'm going to do what makes sense for the story."

"This isn't about you, or your story. This is about operational safety." He pulls me back against his hard body, his lips right next to my ear. "You've got two choices, Mary. You submit to my punishment when we get back, or I put your ass on the next plane back to the United States."

"You can't do that!"

"Watch me." He releases me, gives me enough space to turn around. I guess he thinks he's made his point. He's wrong.

"You're not sending me anywhere." I get in his face, just like he's getting in mine. He doesn't need to hold my head up to his, because I was never going to back down to him anyway. "I'm here because you were ordered to take me, so how about YOU start following your orders, and stop trying to turn me into your bitch."

I can feel his powerful body less than an inch away from mine. I can see the frustration and anger coursing through him. He doesn't get me at all. It's not my job to hunker down in the back and wait for the good guys to protect me. It's my job to go and see what the bad guys are doing.

"If these men take you, what happened to you in that laboratory is going to look like a summer camp," he growls. "I can see you've got a death wish, but you're not dying on my watch."

"I don't have a death wish. A death wish would be sitting in the back of the biggest potential target in the village and waiting for you to come back having achieved nothing at all. I'm entitled to talk to people. It's literally what I'm here for."

"I don't give a fuck what you think you're here for, or what you think you're entitled to," he snarls down at me. "You do as I damn well say."

"Uh, sir? We need to get moving."

A reluctant voice comes from outside the vehicle. It gets through to Ken in a way nothing I have said does and makes us both realize that we're basically having a domestic spat in the middle of an Afghani village. Not a good look for anybody.

"Let's go!" Ken calls out. I slink to the back and stay as far away from him as possible as we head out of the village and back to the FOB.

The ride back to base is slow and stony silent, on my part anyway. I'm not pleased with the way he dragged me away like he owns me. I'm not exactly an embedded reporter if I have to sit inside the car like a little kid every time we stop.

Ken's protectiveness is out of line and way over the top, and we are going to have words, just as soon as they're not in front of all his buddies who I know will back him up. Everyone is subdued and quiet. They didn't find their gun runners and they obviously didn't get the information they wanted in the village either. So this isn't my fault, strictly. This is tired men being grumpy because the heat of the day is coming on now and we're all starting to gently bake.

The smell of sweat, socks, and opened MREs starts

to pervade the vehicle, amplified by masculine farts. I'd ask to have a window opened, but something tells me they're not going to add ventilation just for me.

KEN

"Sit the hell down, before I tie you down," I growl as she lifts her ass off the seat to try to look out the sliver of reinforced window. This isn't going to be a sight-seeing tour for her now.

She is in serious trouble. She wandered off out of line of sight. Anything could have happened to her. It takes less than a second for a hidden terrorist to pop out and slit someone's throat. It's happened before. Not everyone in the villages is friendly, and not every person who wears a hijab is a woman either. It was a simple instruction and she outright disobeyed it.

Fortunately, there's a good long drive to calm down in, and plan what I'm going to do with her. If she was in the military, she'd be getting chewed the hell out and punished severely with the sort of shit work and PT that'd break her will and leave her in a state to actually learn something.

I don't want to break her down. Life has already had a damn good go at that, and it didn't work. Not everyone is made for military handling. A lot of people will crumple so bad they'll never go back together again. And some are so hard, either through natural temperament or life experience that being ripped to shreds and humiliated just doesn't touch them. I shudder to think what it would take to get Mary into a receptive frame of mind now. She's no baby rookie who can be shouted into cowering submission. I've got to go against my instincts and put a lot of what I learned over the years to the side. Even if she is a little different from the usual personnel I deal with, she can be trained, and she damn well will be. I will not let her put herself into the kind of danger she was just in again. We've had soldiers taken by 'villagers' before. Some of these fighters are opportunists. They can blend in with the innocent locals seamlessly. A lot of them genuinely are locals, so the danger we're in is not understated. That's why we go in armed, and in sufficient numbers to defend ourselves. And it's why we don't wander around asking vague questions about husbands and nonsense like that. This is Afghanistan, not a college canteen.

I can feel her eyes on me. She doesn't seem sorry in the slightest yet, but she will be.

When we get back to base, I dismiss the others. Macky and Fraser are both good guys, but they won't keep their mouths shut about that little incident. I've got to get Mary under control, and quick.

"Come with me," I say, my tone clipped but controlled.

She follows me back to the CHU, a sulky, quiet expression on her face. She's wary. I open the door and stand outside, refraining from the impulse to smack her ass hard as she walks past me into the cabin.

"Fine, so you're mad," she says in a fairly transparent attempt to get ahead of the discussion. That's not going to happen.

I take her by the arm and push her gently, but firmly against the wall. Her eyes spit fire, her teeth are clenched. She's ready to fight me because she still doesn't understand. This isn't about me being an overbearing asshole. It's not some bruised ego because she didn't obey me. This is literally life and death. Her life and potentially, her death.

MARY

He's so fucking tall. It's not possible that he's taller when he's angry, but he seems taller right now, his hands on either side of my head, but higher as he leans over me, looming shamelessly.

I know he doesn't want me to be aroused by this. I don't want to be aroused by this, but he's wearing short sleeves and his biceps are ripping over my head and he's hot when he's angry. The intensity which is always present lurking beneath the surface of his controlled exterior bursts forth. I can feel it emanating from him, pure masculine energy pumping into the space between us.

I'm tingling with excitement, my heart is pounding.

"I was doing my job!" I offer the excuse, knowing he's not going to accept it.

"You were maybe sixty seconds from being sushi," he growls. "That village isn't safe. We're pretty sure it's being used as a stopover for weapons trafficking.

There's every chance that those houses hide stockpiles of ammunition, explosives, god knows what else. When you're out here, everybody is a possible threat. There are fighters everywhere. Do you know what would happen to you if they got hold of you? Shall I get descriptive, Mary? Do you want to know what they do to women they capture?"

"I've had worse."

Those three words hit him square between the eyes, because they're delivered with the weight of truth. I have seen worse. Far worse. I see worse when I close my eyes. I know the reputation for brutality and cruelty some of the fighters have out here, but I have seen creative cruelty played out in ways that would make the men out here cringe. I refuse to be frightened of that anymore.

"Then use your damn brain," he growls. "You think I want to find pieces of you?"

"What do you care?"

I throw the question at him, and his head rocks back as if I hit him.

"What do I care?" He growls the question again, shaking his head. He seems surprised, and maybe even a little hurt. I guess he's forgotten the same thing I keep forgetting. We don't really know each other. We're total strangers, and whatever bond we do have was forged in such a fucked up way I don't know if it will ever be strong enough to support anything remotely resembling a healthy relationship.

Right now, that's not what's at issue though. Right

now, he just wants control. Control I don't want to give anybody, even him.

I can see him hunting for words inside his mind. I don't know what he's going to say, and in the end he says nothing. His mouth descends on mine in a passionate kiss which captures my lips and makes all thought of resistance flee my mind. His lips are strong, but soft, urging mine apart and soon his tongue is snaking against mine. Our kiss deepens. His hands move from the wall and cup my head, large paws cradling me as he kisses me with the kind of passion I have only felt inside myself, the sort no man has ever mustered for me before.

I breathe him. Taste him. Feel him. My world is him and I am his as my tongue twirls with his and returns the vigor of desire.

When he breaks the kiss, none of the intensity has been lost.

"You're going to do as you're told," he says in a husky growl. "I don't care if you want to. I don't care if you understand why you need to. I'm going to make sure you do either way."

"You're going to spank me again?"

"I'm going to do more than spank you, girl," he promises. "I'm going to strip you down and…"

"No!"

My voice is strained and panicked.

"No?"

"You can spank me. You can even fuck me. But you can't see me naked."

He tilts his head to the side, and a look of compassion comes into his eyes. I don't want that look. I don't want pity. I want his anger, his fury, his passion. I want him to want me so fiercely that I forget the reason I can't be nude with him.

"I'm going to have you naked," he says, softly, but firmly.

Emotion cascades inside me. Fear. Relief. Both so intimately entwined and neither one of them making sense in tandem with the other. The relief is that it is no longer my call to make. The fear is that he will see what they did to me and then this moment will evaporate forever. Men don't want broken women. They want whole creatures, perfect nubile, fertile goddesses. I'm barely female anymore. He doesn't know that yet. But he will when he takes my clothes off.

I stand there, waiting for him to tear my secrets from me, but instead of those powerful hands ripping at zippers and buttons, he takes two steps back and looks at me.

"Strip."

What? I can't.

"Mary," he says, his voice more firm than ever. "Take your clothes off. Now."

"I can't." My voice shakes and cracks. "I can't..."

All I can do right now is repeat those two words. I can't take my clothes off. I can't let him see me. I can't be naked. I can't. I can't. I can't. I'm frozen and useless to him and to myself.

Ken makes a soft sound and steps forward.

"What are you afraid of?"

I can't even bring myself to say it. I want to cry. I'm ruining this. He wanted me. He was going to have me. If I weren't so fucked up and broken he'd probably be inside me right now. Instead, I'm cowering before him and trying to hide the tears which are coming to my eyes.

Ken's arms slide around me. He sweeps me up against his body and carries me over to his bed. He lays me down and lowers his body next to mine, his arms encircling my waist as he pulls me up to rest against him. Then he holds me close as I bury my face in his chest and wish I wasn't like this.

"Whatever you're afraid of... I promise, it won't come true," he rumbles with reassurance.

It's a big promise, and one he shouldn't be making.

"I'm ruined, Ken. Forever. No man is ever going to want me."

"That is absolutely not true," he says, his voice low and serious.

I turn my face away from him. He doesn't understand. He's an incredible man and an amazing person. He's brave, he's incredibly smart, and he's one of the most physically powerful people I've ever met. He could have literally any woman he wanted. He could walk into a grocery store and pick a woman up like most people pick up a few apples.

"Mary." He growls my name and a ripple of delicious fear runs down my spine. Yes, I am afraid of him, but fear has a different meaning to me now. This fear I feel with him is nothing like the horror I endured in the hospital. That was a death of feeling which drained me of my will to exist. The fear I feel with him makes me more alive, causes my heart to race, my tummy to flutter. Little goosebumps appear on my skin, and the hair on the back of my next stands erect.

"Look at me."

I can barely bring myself to look at him. He makes me shy. He is everything a man should be. I am nothing a woman should be and we both know it.

"Look at me!" He snaps the words with harsh command and when I still don't move my head, he takes my chin and turns my head toward him.

"You are beautiful," he says. "You are not less for what you have been through. You are more. You bear the scars of life. That's nothing to be ashamed of. They are marks which tell everyone who sees them how much you have survived."

"Men don't care what a woman has survived. They want a pretty little innocent unblemished girl. They want to be the ones to defile. They don't want used, broken women."

I see a flash of pure anger in his eyes. "And who taught you that?"

"Everyone?" I shrug. I know it's true. They don't advertise cars with scantily clad women covered in scars and marks.

"Not all men are mindless, and not all men are looking for an innocent princess," he says. "Don't give up on love yet."

He pulls his fingers away from my chin and lets me sit with those words. They're nice, but it's going to take more than words to change how I feel inside.

"I'm going to take your clothes off you, Mary," he says. "I'm going to start now. You can stop me if you want to, but I don't want you to."

I lie there next to him as his fingers find the zipper at the top of my neck and lower it down to my waist in a slow, steady motion. That alone won't bare anything. Beneath the overalls, I have a white t-shirt and a bra on top, and boxers and panties below. I left him remove the overalls, feeling their heavy protection slide away from me.

"Lay on your back," he urges softly, crouching over me as he pulls the thick fabric from my hips and down off my legs.

I'm letting him do what he wants with me, and I don't even know why. Maybe part of me just wants to get his rejection over with. He's not going to want me once he sees me, I know that much.

His fingers curl under my t-shirt, peel it up an inch and I freeze. Now he can see them for sure, the little white lines marking me. He doesn't hesitate, doesn't even seem to see them as he draws it up, over my head. I can't see him for a moment. There is nothing but white fabric, pit sweat in the underarms and then I am free, in my bra.

"They're everywhere," I say as he puts a strong hand to my belly, his splayed fingers running over my skin. "They kept… they…" I can't begin to say what they did.

He can see what they did. Every part of it is written in scar tissue, perfectly neat, anal retentive marks joining and converging across my torso.

He's looking at me. Seeing me as I really am. Scars and all. I can't read the expression on his face and I don't know if I want to either. Does he pity me? Is he disgusted?

The fear has gone. It's been replaced with something almost worse: safety.

I can't risk feeling this safe. That makes no sense to anyone who hasn't been hurt, but it's the most urgent thing in my mind. I have to get up, away from his strong arms. I have to hide myself away, make sure that he doesn't have the chance to love me.

"Stay still." His voice is gruff, and stern and calm. It gentles me. And then he reaches for my bra, his fingers finding the clasp between my breasts. This is the moment of truth.

KEN

Her left nipple is missing. There's a thin line of scar tissue where it once was. It's not as bad as it could be, and plenty of people live with far worse, but I know none of that matters because it's all an abstract concept until it's your body and it's happening to you.

I cup her breast and run my fingers over her skin.

"You're beautiful," I say. I mean it too. She is beautiful in so many ways. She's strong and she's soft and she's the kind of woman who is capable of challenging me without being a raging harridan about it. She's the perfect mixture of bratty girl and mature, driven woman. She doesn't really need me. She would survive on her own just fine, but I want to be there for her. I want to make sure she never hurts like this again.

"You're just saying that because you have to."

"I don't have to say a goddamn thing, girl," I growl, leaning down and nipping lightly at her earlobe. She's going to learn a new relationship with pain with me. She's going to learn that it can hurt good. It can be constructive, and instructive.

"They defaced me."

"They left their marks. I left a few marks on them too," I say, my lip curling back in feral instinct at the memory. Very occasionally, it is good to unleash the animal which prowls at the back of every male mind, the thing which craves blood and death and the screams of the dying. I was a beast the day I took her from them, and I do not regret a moment of it.

I run my hands down her body, the curves of her waist and hips and I find the underwear which is keeping the rest of her from me. It slides down her body at my urging, leaving her utterly bare besides dark curls at the very apex of her thighs.

The scars truly aren't as terrible as she has imagined them to be, but she won't believe me, not yet. She's lying there with fear in her beautiful eyes because she can't risk believing what I'm saying to her.

So I pull my shirt off. Let her see the man she is with. I bear the marks of war. Three bullet holes. One in my right shoulder, another below my ribs, the third an inch lower. I caught six bullets that day, these strays were the ones that missed the vest. There's also a long burn from an explosion which runs down the left-hand side of my abdominal plane.

"I'm hardly untouched either," I point out, lifting her hands to my body, so she can run her fingers over my torso and the scars that mark it.

The military is a massive organism which, among other things, has become expert in the application of pain and damage. But those skills can be used to heal as well as to hurt.

"It's different for men. Men are supposed to be scarred."

I raise a brow as I look down at her. "Miss Mary, you wouldn't be sexist would you?"

She gives me a little smirk of a smile, and a hint of a laugh. My heart swells at her reaction. She is letting me in, and she is beautiful. She is the most beautiful woman in the world, scars or not, I can see her pain and her bravery, her strength and her softness. They are all laid bare to me.

I lower my head and begin to kiss her body, every part of her I can. This is reconnaissance. I am learning where she squirms, where she moans, where she goes soft and gives little gasps.

My cock is rock hard and I want nothing more than to push it between her thighs where her dark curls are hiding the entrance to her tight pussy, but I take my time. Because I want to, and because I know it must have been a very long time since she was with a man. Her fear of showing those scars tells me all I need to know.

"Please," she whimpers. "I need you inside me."

I don't like to disappoint a lady, especially not one as beautiful as she is. It's my pleasure to push the head of my cock to that heated, wet little crevice between her legs and surge forward, feeling her body wrap around me in perfect feminine embrace.

I take it slowly, make sure she isn't in any pain. She is very tight and her body takes some time to adjust, but soon she is moving back against me with little moans which don't hold those first whimpers of pain, and soon I am lost in her body, surging back and forth inside her hot, wet little cunt.

She's perfect. I can't express how gorgeous she is, how her body and her character and her fucking soul are all so beautiful to me as I rock my hips against her, supporting my upper body on my arms so I can look down and enjoy the sight of her.

It's not long before I am seeing past the scars entirely. They are a small part of the total package, the curve of her hip, the softness of her thighs, the way her tongue curls against mine as I kiss her deeply.

I wanted to fuck her, but I am making love to her, and in this moment it feels as though we have known each other for lifetimes.

It's so good, I almost forget. Almost.

"I was going to punish you, wasn't I?"

She undulates beneath me, her inner walls

squeezing my cock, her hot wet embrace driving me to distraction. I can't let her make me forget. She was a disobedient little brat and she will pay for that.

I slide my cock out of her, admire the way her pussy lips flower so beautifully, pink and spread and dewy with her arousal and mine.

She can't think that she's going to get away with things because of scars, or ideology, or any other excuse she throws at me in hopes of getting away with things. She's going to pay for her disobedience the old-fashioned way.

"Face down on the bed."

She makes a whimpering sound, but it's heated and it's soft and when she rolls over I see the pretty curve of her yet to be reddened cheeks. She has a great ass. It's full and feminine. I could stare at it all day, but right now I'm going to lay my belt across it and make damn sure she knows that when I say stay, I mean **stay.**

I stand up, my cock bobbing erect and covered in the sleek shine of her juices. I go for my belt, two inches of nice thick shiny black leather, a perfect contrast to the pale ass she's presenting to me.

"In the future, you're going to be a good girl and do as I say, aren't you," I murmur, reaching down to stroke her hair.

"Yessir," she mumbles.

I'm pretty sure she'd say anything to get my cock back inside her. I can tell from the way she's rolling that ass she's not even thinking about the belt. She wants that tight inner hole filled. Soon. Once I'm done teaching her a lesson.

MARY

The belt lands across my ass, a searing stroke which makes heat flash deep through my flesh. Holy fuck, he's really taking his belt to me. I feel like one of the little rascals or something, caught by daddy and taking a licking for it. The thought makes me giggle just as the next stroke lands and my giggle turns into a gasp.

"You think this is funny, huh?"

He stands over me, so sexy and dominant, the leather clutched between his big hands.

"No?" I squeak the answer. I don't think this is funny at all.

Other people have hurt me, but this isn't pain in the way they inflicted it. This is the kind of heat and sting which wraps around my soul and makes me feel held. This is the kind of pain that imposes a limit, not the pain that degrades and destroys.

This... is what I have been searching for all this time. I didn't know it. I just kept pushing and pushing, looking for this feeling. This safety which is not entirely safe, this affection that isn't cloying, shallow nonsense delivered with a plastic bag of wilting flowers and a dinner at a lobster chain.

"You're going to follow orders," he snaps, his voice holding just the right note of dominance and care. "I will not let you get hurt because you think you know better. I will not let harm come to you from anyone, including yourself."

I need him. Not because of fate, but because he alone in the world seems to be able to see me for what I am. He doesn't look past the scars. He understands them. He's not afraid of them, or what they mean, and he doesn't pity me for having them. They're not a get out of jail free card for me either. In spite of seeing what lies beneath my clothes, the marks of those who hurt me so deeply I never thought I would heal, he's willing to whip my ass because I disobeyed him, and maybe that means he intends to have me with him long enough for that obedience to matter.

The belt lands a dozen more times, hot strokes making my ass burn. It all feels good. The arousal he left me with when he pulled out of me still burns low in my belly and the lashes of the leather that should hurt like hell are transformed into pure erotic energy.

He drops the belt and surges inside me, his cock plunging deep into my soaking wet pussy. I let out a cry of pleasure as an incredible sensation washes through me. His strong arms wrap around me, draw me up from the bed, push me back against the wall and I am pinned there as his powerful hips surge against me time and time again, his mouth on my neck, my breasts, my lips, devouring me.

This is not fucking, or lovemaking, this is something deeper and more satisfying than either of those things, and it is both combined. We are the same thing, for several incredible minutes, there is no difference between he and me. His cock plunges inside me, is wrapped in the tight embrace of my inner walls and we are one.

Orgasm comes like a wild thing, rushing through us, making our blood boil. The thrusting, the crying out, the rough grinding and the desperate clenching, the tightening of muscles and the spending of seed. He carries me through it all until I can barely breathe from pleasure, and then he draws me back down to the messy bed where we began and we lie together in a silent reverie in which there are no words, only touch.

4
———

MARY

Fast asleep in Ken's arms, I feel as if nothing can touch me. I have never been as safe as this. Not ever, in my entire life have I felt so completely secure and utterly protected. He has touched me in ways no man has, he's made orgasm something damn near transcendent. For the first time in a long time, I don't feel damaged, or broken, or scarred. I feel complete.

Later on, I'll learn that it was 02:39 when the alarms went off. In deep sleep, it's a detail I miss completely. All I know is that it's loud and the arms which have been cradling me all night suddenly aren't there anymore.

Are we under attack?

Ken is up and out of the CHU in a second, with only a hasty "STAY" thundered at me. How he managed to get clothes and boots on that fast, I have no idea. It's as if he magicked them on before I could properly wake up.

I know better than to leave the room, but I get up and get dressed too, a lot slower than he did, but I want to be prepared in case we have to move. Bases like this one are vulnerable. There are jihadi forces spread across the country, some loyal to Isil, others only to their respective warlords. It's impossible to truly explain how fractured this country is. It's not just this war which has made things unpleasant. There are hatreds here which go back centuries, long before the empires which ripped this land apart were even dreamt of, let alone founded.

My impression of the efforts to tame this place is that they are futile. Not because peace is impossible, but because the tapestry of this place is more complex than we can handle. There's nuance and depth. To understand even one village, you would have to spend a good year hearing the stories, learning brothers of brothers, mothers of mothers.

I think about all of this as I sit on the bed and wait to find out what's happening. There could be a mortar incoming at this very moment. I'd never know it hit, unless it hit just far enough away to rip through the wall of this thing and turn the alloy into shards which burst through the human body like a thousand tiny hot knives. Best not to think about it really, but hard not to.

Sitting and waiting to die, hoping I won't, I'm at peace. Ken is out there. I don't know what he's doing, but the anxiety which would usually be making me a nervous wreck just isn't there. He'll take care of me. I mean, as far as he can, even he can't do anything about an incoming shell.

I walk to the door and open it a fraction, just so I can see what's going on. The base is in serious motion, armored vehicles are being deployed, but I don't hear gun fire, which means the base itself isn't being assaulted. The fighting must be happening somewhere else. Somewhere that matters.

I close the door and go back to my bed. It's cool and neat because it hasn't been laid in yet tonight. I abandoned it for Ken's arms and I don't regret it for a second.

What if he doesn't come back?

The question forces itself into my mind. What if he doesn't? He might not. War takes the good and the brave and the talented. It does not discriminate in its swathes of destruction. Even the most agile fighters can be caught off-balance. Even the stealthiest spies can be exposed.

All I can do is wait and hope. Hope that he comes back safe. Hope that the fighting stays distant. Hope that we survive another day. I lie there looking at the ceiling, not awake, not asleep, just floating in that place insomniacs know all too well.

The sun is up when he returns. He smells. It's a stench of human misery and burning flesh. It's the sort of scent you don't get off your clothes. You throw them the hell away.

I stay still, pretend to be asleep as he tramps to the shower. I hear the water go on, and his clothes hit the ground. If this was anywhere else in the world, any other time, I'd try to go and join him, but the smell he brought with him is pervading the CHU ever more thickly, curling into my nasal passages, making me want to vomit. I can't stay in here with that smell. I push off the bed and throw open the door, gasping for fresh air as I stand back against the CHU. There are men and women everywhere, going about their business with grim, tired faces.

From here, I can see that some of the vehicles have taken damage. Charred, twisted metal has been towed back to the FOB. Jesus. The place is a hive of activity. I'd love to go and get a closer look, but I'm not really supposed to be out here at all, and I can see enough to get a sense of the atmosphere anyway. It's tense, but professional. These men and women work with the ferocity and alacrity of fire ants, mending what needs to be mended, tending to those that need it. It's really impressive to watch, training turning to effective action which makes the worst conditions in the world not just survivable, but winnable.

"What are you doing out here?" Ken's gruff tones interrupt my thoughts.

"Breathing," I answer as I turn around to see him standing in the doorway, a white towel around his waist. "Are you okay?"

I don't know if I'm in trouble, and I don't care. I just want to know that he's alright.

"I'm fine. Thought I told you to stay inside," he says, crossing his arms over his chest and looking down at me with that patchwork stare of his.

"I.. the smell…"

"Yeah, sorry," he says. "I got rid of most of it."

You don't really get rid of it, not right away anyway. It's pervading the camp, light on the breeze, but present. Indescribably here.

"Did anyone get hurt?" I ask the question maybe more bluntly than I need to. There's no good way to ask it, and Ken's never given me the feeling I need to mince words with him.

"Couple wounded on our side. Nothing life ending."

"And on theirs?"

"They're still counting. I'll leave this door open, but come inside."

He ushers me back indoors and I go. This is the reality of life out here. At any minute of the day or night, you can be ripped from your life and sent to end someone else's. I feel guilty for being relieved that he is okay, and that all "our side" are okay, while out there, not so far away, there are a lot of people who are very much not okay at all.

Before my stint in the hospital, I would never have

been able to handle this. It took away so many things, but it gave me one or two things too - like an understanding of what it truly means to have an enemy, a deep knowing that there are people in the world who will do unspeakable harm. Not in aid of a goal, necessarily, but just because they can.

It's a fine line between necessary violence and outright sadism, and in the end it is simply a matter of character. Weak men take pleasure in hurting others, they give in to the beast inside which bays for blood, and the demon which laughs at cruelty. Strong men can do necessary violence without glee. They do it because it is necessary, and they are even more frightening in some ways than the sadists, because their actions are calculated, clear, and devastatingly effective.

"I'm sorry you had to go do that."

He gives me a curious little smile. "It's my job," he says. "Someone had to do it, and seeing as I'm more or less on loan out here, I'm happy to do what I can to increase safety."

"You're not with your unit?"

Stupid question really. I would have noticed a special forces unit here for sure. They carry themselves differently, for better and for worse. Ken is something of a sore thumb in some ways.

"No," he says. "I'm out here doing some solo reconnaissance, with backup from these guys. Once I achieve that goal, I'm due leave."

Leave. So he'll be gone. I'll miss him. The thought of

him not being around is already like a knife to the guts, but I try not to dwell on that. We have however long we have together and that will just have to be enough. If there's one thing life has taught me, it's that nothing is forever.

"When you came for me in the hospital, you weren't special forces then, were you?"

"I was between enlistments."

That makes sense. Men like him are rare and valuable to the military. It's not uncommon for them to take breaks between enlistments, or even to think that they're done, only to return. It's a calling.

"I'm really lucky you were," I say softly. If not for him… that doesn't bear thinking about either. My thoughts are like a minefield of things better not confronted. Sometimes it's hard to think at all with all the things I can't think about.

"We never talked about what happened there," he says, gently probing. "How you came to be there…"

I guess I owe him some answers. It's literally the least I can give him.

"I was poking my nose in where I wasn't wanted," I say with a rueful ghost of what might be a smile. "I'd heard that there were remnants of certain groups continuing the work of their forefathers in South America. I thought maybe I should investigate. I got some funding from an indie news network and I went out there."

"Alone?"

"Yeah, they only paid me enough to go alone. Said if

I found anything, they'd up the budget for the story. But that never happened obviously, because I got caught the first week I was down there. I had managed to sneak up through the hospital, find the wings that obviously weren't treatment wings." I talk quickly and blankly, trying desperately not to recall the emotion associated with the incident. "I thought they would maybe beat me up and throw me out, or worst case scenario, kill me. But they managed to find a worse option."

"A lot of strings were pulled to get you out of there," he says. "You must be connected in some pretty high places."

"I have no connections," I say, shaking my head. "I guess I just got lucky."

"You never found out who got you out? I thought…"

Shit. He's asking a lot of specific questions now. I force myself to stay as calm as possible, though it's fucking hard.

"What?"

"I thought it was your family who had tracked you down," he says with a slight frown.

"I was an only child to a single mother, and my mother died while I was in there," I say, trying not to let the sadness overwhelm me. "When I got back 'home' I didn't have anyone, or anything. I was missing, presumed dead. So they cleared out my apartment and sold my stuff. My friends had moved on. Scared a shit out of a couple of them though."

"Oh yeah?" The corner of his lip twists with amusement.

"Turns out, my being dead was real convenient for my boyfriend and best friend. They were so heartbroken about it all that by the time I saw them again, they were together."

"Ouch," Ken grimaces.

"And they had a one month old baby."

"Oh god." He rolls his eyes and shakes his head.

"Yeah, the guy was so sad about me he knocked her up a couple months after I was gone. So, no. There wasn't anyone in my personal life looking for me, that's for sure. Actually, after a few weeks of being back, I realized…" I hesitate for a second. "I realized that life had gone on without me. So I got my press credentials, and I headed out here."

"Shit," he says, reaching for me and pulling me into a hug against his bare upper body. He's rippling with hard won muscles as I curl into his protective embrace.

This man has been up all night fighting. He came home wearing the scent of the dead. And yet he's comforting me right now. I don't know whether to be touched by that, or to feel like an asshole for making this all about me. Both, really.

"It's okay," I mumble into his chest. "I'm safe now."

"Goddamn right you are," he says, squeezing me tight. "Did you get any sleep when I was gone?"

"A bit."

"So none," he says. "Come on."

He lays back on the bed, clad in nothing but the

towel and I curl up into him. The door stands slightly ajar, kept open with a boot to allow the dusty breeze to pass into the CHU. It's already warm and it's going to get hotter, but I close my eyes and I press my face against his body, and I take what I can get for this moment, right now.

5

MARY

A few days pass. It's quiet for the most part and Ken and I spend the time together, mostly in bed. He is a demanding and dominant lover. I am a rebellious and receptive one. Together, we are incandescent with passion. In this world of death and fury, mating has a greater meaning and more satisfaction. He is a lion in bed, his cock surging in an out of my aching cunt. I'm sore from sex, but I want more. Always more.

Work inevitably calls again though, work I am allowed to accompany him on. Something relatively boring then, though I don't mind because it means I will be with him.

"We're going to roll through that same village we did the other day," he says as we head out. "I want you to stay in the vehicle. Tensions are high right now."

"Why?"

"That attack the other night originated from a local warlord. They're trying to move in over this way, and the villagers are loyal to them already. But he's a nasty son of a bitch and I want him. He knows that. So it was this village he hit that night. It's a warning, to us, to stay away. They'll be punished with death if they don't resist us. So today could be dodgy. Stay in the car, no matter what you see, and no matter what happens."

"Okay, I agree. "No problem."

"That was easy," he says, his brow raised in surprise.

I'm surprised too. I want to please him. It's a strange impulse for a woman like me, but I guess I'll get used to it.

The first part of our journey is relatively uneventful. There are more burned out vehicles on the side of the road than before, some of them no doubt from the battle a few days ago. I usually don't have much of a reaction to sights like these, but on this occasion I'm reminded that Ken was in the middle of this. He was in the range of fire, he was exposed to all this death and destruction. It's the water in which he swims. I always knew that about him, but this is the first time I really feel it, and it's the first time it upsets me.

As we enter the village, there are more sights which indicate battle has taken place. Some of the houses have been utterly destroyed. Others are burned out. There is more chaos than there was last time, and as we roll through, the villagers are obviously suspicious. I try to keep an eye out for the women I met last time, just to see if they're okay.

Ken stops the convoy, takes a couple of guys with him and steps out. I wait in the back, two other soldiers with me, weapons at the ready. There's a little window I can look out of and I see the chaos in the village at close quarters.

Somewhere, in the midst of the shuffle and the work to rebuild, I see a man and a woman fighting. Well, a woman who is cowering and a man who is yelling at her. As they draw closer I see that it is one of the women from my first visit. I also see that he has, in his hand, one of the little soaps I gave out then. The context is immediately clear. She is being harassed and hurt because of me, because she wanted something a little nice.

In her, I see myself. I see how I was hurt in that laboratory. I couldn't fight back, and she isn't fighting back either, because to do so would be to guarantee her own death.

I see the man's fist rise and come down toward the woman. Everything becomes slow motion.

I'll never be able to explain what happens next.

It's pure rage, and it animates me without my conscious will.

The sliver of mind which watches my actions dispassionately notes that I am running from the LAV. I am shouting at the top of my lungs. I am lashing out with boots and fists and before I know it the man who was trying to beat the woman is on the ground and I am hitting him with every bit of fury and strength I have.

KEN

"Jesus Christ!"

It takes three of us to pull Mary off the guy. He's hiding his face in the sand, covering his head with his hands and she is going in on him like a feral animal. There is shouting and chaos and weapons are being drawn and guns cocked and for fuck's sake this situation was like a powder keg when we rolled up here and now it's turned into a dangerous farce.

We grab Mary and throw her into the LAV none too gently. There's no time for gentle. I bark at the others to hold her in there and I do my best to settle the situation, which has devolved into chaos. It soon becomes apparent that there is no hope of salvaging this mess. If we don't want to get into an armed conflict, we need to get out of here.

"Back to base. Now!"

It's a retreat, and a shameful one on multiple levels. I am pissed.

Mary sits in the back of the LAV, a rebellious expression on her face.

As much as what she did seems admirable, it wasn't. It was stupid as hell. The guy she went for is the cousin of the man I'm looking for. He's an asshole, but he was on the verge of giving me some information. Now there's not a man in that village who will work with us. She just humiliated someone they respect, and she humiliated us too. It's sexist, but a woman who can't be controlled is one of the most offensive things to these people. We lost face, we lost ground, we lost intel. And now, I'm going to lose her.

I take Mary off the LAV and to my CHU as soon as it stops inside the base. She stays quiet, brimming with fury for the fight we both know we're about to have.

"He was hitting her!"

Sure enough, she practically explodes the moment we get inside.

"I don't care if he shot her, you don't attack people out here," I growl. She doesn't get it. She's a huge danger to herself and to everybody else, and I can't allow that.

"I'm sending you home. Your credentials are in the process of being revoked." Saying those words hurts me. It's fucking awful, but there's no other option.

"What?" Her eyes go wide.

"I can't let you run amok out here, Mary. You almost got every single one of us killed, and I guarantee you that woman's life wasn't improved by what you did either. You're impulsive and you're reckless and you're a danger to yourself and everyone around you. Pack your stuff. You're going home."

"I don't have a fucking home!"

"You'll find one, Mary."

I don't want to send her away. I want to keep her with me, but this is no place for a woman like her. I have to send her home to save her. It's the hardest fucking thing I've ever had to do, and every part of me wants to go back with her, but I can't. She has to go. And she has to go alone.

"So you fucked me and now you're done with me. I get it."

She makes everything worse with that accusation which devalues everything we've ever had.

"Don't you dare," I growl right back at her. "I want you, Mary. I goddamn well fucking love you, but you are not in the right frame of mind to be out here, and I'm not going to risk it anymore. You're going back."

"Fuck you, Ken."

I see the rejection and anger in her eyes. I'm sure she hates me in this moment. If I have to be hated to keep her safe, then that's what I'll be. The next chopper out of here leaves in two hours, and her ass is going to be on it.

———

The next hours are some of the worst I've had in a long time. I wanted so much for her to be able to stay with me until I get leave. I wanted to take her somewhere nice, Singapore maybe, or a beach in Thailand. But that's not going to be possible now.

She needs help. The kind of help I can't give her here. Her emotions get the best of her, and no matter what she says, I know a death wish when I see one.

For a second time, I find myself putting the woman I want above all others onto a helicopter.

"Be good, Mary."

She refuses to even look at me as she gets aboard. Her face is a cold mask. She's hurt. So am I.

We'll survive.

6

___

MARY

I feel like shit. I feel worse than shit, because I know I deserve this, and I know I basically made him do this to me. It's too late to apologize as the chopper lifts me into the sky. He's done with me. And it's all my fault.

The journey back to the States is long and miserable. I don't have anything waiting for me there. He knows that, but it's not his problem. I'm not his problem. I'm absolutely crushed, surrounded by soldiers who are excited to be going home.

They will be held on base for a week or two to acclimate when they return. I'll be left at the airport. Fucked if I know what I'll do then, maybe grab a cheap motel for the night before I explain to my editor how I got expelled.

I'm alone again. For one single week, I wasn't alone. I had someone. I felt like I had something. And then I fucked it all up. I was so angry when he sent me away, and I still am, but I know it's my fault. He can't babysit me and fight a war at the same time, and something about being near someone who cares about me makes me more reactive and less controlled.

I've been holding onto sanity for a long time, just by the skin of my teeth. I don't know what I'm going to do now. I don't know what I'm going to do for work. I don't know where I'm going to live. I have nobody and nothing and I don't want this flight to end, because once it does, I will be truly and completely alone.

All I'm hoping for now is being able to keep it together long enough to get to a motel before I absolutely break down.

LAX is a weird place to be. A perpetual transition zone. I don't want to get off the plane. I don't want to go through customs. But I do all of it because I have to. And then, all around me, there are dozens of families surging forward to greet their loved ones home from war. It's beautiful, and I am glad for them, but so miserable for myself I can barely breathe.

Winding my way through the crowds, I make my way to the doors which lead out to the cab ranks. God I can't wait to be alone. As I walk, I see one man standing near the exit. He's holding a sign with my name on it. Well, not my name. *Ms Brown.* That could be anyone's name. I glance at him, and realize how familiar he looks, even though I've certainly never met him before. He's handsome for sure, and the hard lines of his face remind me of Ken. I don't want to be reminded of Ken. I look away and keep walking.

"Mary Brown?"

He says my name as I walk past. I ignore him. I don't want to talk to anyone who knows I'm here. That can't be good news.

"Mary…"

I look over my shoulder. He's following me across the airport. Jesus. What the hell is going on? I consider heading toward security, just in case something is about to go wrong.

"Ken sent me, Mary."

Ken's name makes anger and shame flash through me. "Ares doesn't have any authority to send anyone for me."

"Hey, easy," he says, reaching out to stop me in my tracks. "I'm Tom. I'm Ken's brother."

"Shit, sorry to hear that."

I try to walk away again, but his grip tightens on my arm.

"Now settle down, little girl, I'm here to pick you up and take you home. Ken asked me to."

"Oh he did huh?" I lift my jaw and stare at him angrily, meanwhile, on the inside, I'm melting. Did he really send his brother to get me? Does he actually still care? I mean, it's still fucked up because he didn't say a damn thing to me about it, but then again I refused to speak to him at all once he said he was sending me home.

"He did," Tom says calmly, with an easy smile I find pretty disarming.

"This is weird as hell," I mumble, shifting my pack. "What's he doing?"

"Just making sure you're alright. Can I take your bag?"

Maybe this is a trap. Maybe I should tell this guy to fuck off and go and get myself that motel room like I planned. But I'm curious, and that curiosity is always my downfall. I want to see what's in store for me, so I swing my pack over at Tom and nod.

"Alright, lead the way, I guess."

His car is out in the lot. Nice car. Don't know what make. Don't care.

We chat on the way to his place. Small talk to cover the fact that he doesn't know me and I don't know him. He asks me a lot of questions I don't really answer, sitting next to this man who reminds me of Ken, but isn't him.

It takes maybe an hour to get out to his place. Tom's house is a modernized bungalow in one of the suburbs. White house, blue trim, a big lawn and a white picket fence. Exactly the kind of place I can't begin to imagine myself living.

I'm not in any position to turn down accommodation though, but still, this is a long way from where I've come from. The sun is shining and there's a gentle breeze. It's fucking beautiful and it makes my stomach churn with nerves. I don't belong here.

"I'm really sorry," I say. "Ken really shouldn't have

told you to come and get me. You know he threw me out, right? Of Afghanistan. He told you to come and get someone who was thrown out of Afghanistan for being too much trouble."

Tom chuckles. He has olive green eyes, I notice, dark hair just like Ken, but his is wavier and longer.

"Your wife isn't going to be pleased you brought me here."

"I'm divorced," he says. "You're free to stay. I'm not worried about how much trouble you'll be."

I don't say anything. Of course he's not worried. People who live in houses like this don't know about trouble. Trouble to them is just drinking a little much, or maybe saying some mean words. Maybe stealing a few twenties. I don't plan on doing any of that, but I know this guy who seems really damn sweet is going to regret having done his brother a favor.

———

He invites me inside. Okay. What the hell. Why not.

The interior is furnished simply, but masculinely. Tom obviously has an IKEA catalog and knows how to use it. I'm not going to complain. Everything is spacious and clean and comfortable. Exactly everything I don't deserve.

"Wow."

"You okay?"

"I just... forgot there's nice stuff in the world, I guess."

He smiles. "Yeah, it's a bit like that, huh. Take a load off. Want some coffee?"

I sit down in a chair, my pack by my side. I'm still so disoriented, but it's nice to be here and not to be alone.

"I'll get out of your hair as soon as I can," I say. "I mean, I'll have to talk to my editor. I'm pretty sure I'm going to get my contract terminated but I still have the story so…"

"You're going to stay," he says, calmly, but firmly. He brings a tray in, coffee, and some cookies too. God. I didn't know how hungry I was.

He's dressed in a green cable knit sweater and blue jeans. Casual and stylish. I'm only getting to look at him properly now I can relax a little. Definitely Ken's brother. Definitely his older brother too.

"I mean I can't stay long," I say. "But thanks for this."

"We'll talk with Ken soon," he says, sitting down on the couch at right angles to the chair.

"I don't really…" I fall silent. I can't exactly say I don't want to talk to Ken, but hell, I really don't. I can't handle talking to him, seeing how much I disappointed him, how bad I was.

"Have something to eat and drink, then go grab a shower." Tom has a way of giving orders too, I notice, though he's a bit more casual about the whole thing. I suspect he means it just as much as Ken would. What have I gotten myself into now?

I nibble at the corner of an oatmeal cookie and try to get my bearings. I'm not in danger. I can tell that much. But I don't know what's going on, not really. I can feel that there's more to this than meets the eye.

———

The room he has for me has a single bed with a pink coverlet. There's something ever so slightly immature about it. I won't complain though. I doubt he has a bunch of spare stuff around for random women his brother expels from the Middle East.

"Thanks. It's really nice."

It is really nice, but it's also really weird. There's a big stuffed bear in the corner. It looks new. If I didn't know better, I'd almost think he bought it for me.

"Is this the room for when your kids come over?"

"No kids," he says. "Now go grab a shower, or a bath if you want one."

A shower sounds good.

———

I don't have much in the way of clothes to change into afterward, but I make do with combat style pants and a white t-shirt. I'm going to need to go shopping, if I can get some money to do it with. I should still be able to sell the story I was putting together in Afghanistan, even with the ignominious end of my tour there.

Once I'm dressed, I pad out to see Tom. He's sitting at the kitchen counter on a laptop. He waves me over to him and points at the screen.

"Someone's been waiting to talk to you."

It's Ken.

His handsome face fills the screen. I want to fucking cry just looking at him. Tears fill my eyes as I try to hold back the emotion which overwhelms me.

"Hi," I manage to squeak out.

"Hey there, little one," he says kindly. "You have a good flight?"

I press my lips together. I don't trust myself to talk.

"I know you're probably shocked as hell right now," he says, "but I meant it when I said you're not going to be alone anymore and you're not going to be left to your own devices. You're mine, Mary, and I'm going to look after you as best I can even if I can't be there with you right now."

I sniff. It's not much of a response.

"I'm going to be responsible for you no matter where you are," he says. "And some day soon, we are going to have a very long conversation in person, young lady."

"You sent me back," I remind him. "You're not in charge of me anymore."

"Nothing has changed between us except the distance."

He's wrong. Everything has changed. He just doesn't want to accept that. He's so damn used to controlling the world. He doesn't get that there are some things so far outside his control that it's laughable. Right now, I'm one of them.

"You sent me away," I say. "You made me come back

here, and it's sweet and all that you got your brother to pick me up, but I don't need discipline and I don't need you. If you wanted me, you could have had me. But you sent me away so…. so…" I find the courage to say what's in my heart… "fuck off."

He's in Afghanistan. He can't do a damn thing to me, and Tom isn't going to do anything either. This is ridiculous.

"You want to come and get me, Ken, you fucking come and get me. I push the laptop closed. That's it. The call ends. He's gone. I push the hollow feeling in my chest away, but I can't stop the hot water trickling down my face.

Fuck him. Fuck him so fucking hard. What a fucking asshole.

I hate that I'm crying. It takes away so much of the vehement self-righteousness of the moment.

Fuck. What am I going to do?

"Come and sit down," Tom says, putting a gentle hand on my shoulder. "You're mentally and emotionally exhausted."

"Yeah, you know me now too?"

"I'm a doctor," he says. "I know the signs."

A doctor. I stiffen with fear. Ken sent me to a fucking doctor's house. What the fuck was he thinking? Instinct takes over. The same instinct that made me rush the guy in the desert sends me bolting for the door in the suburbs. Fuck my stuff. Fuck my laptop. Fuck money. Fuck having anywhere to go. I have to get out of here. I have to get away.

I run into the garden and take deep, panicked breaths. I'm utterly overloaded, deep in panic so intense I feel like I might actually die.

"I take it you don't like doctors," Tom says from behind me.

"Leave me alone!"

"It's okay," he says, seeming unfazed by the scene I'm in the process of making. "No harm's going to come to you. I'm going to be inside okay, when you come in."

"I'm not coming back in. You're a doctor. You're going to try…"

I can't say what he's going to do. It's literally fucking unspeakable.

"I'm going to just be right here, okay," he says, his tone still calm and even. "You're okay, Mary."

I am not okay. I am so far from being okay it's impossible to verbalize it. I can't stand upright. I'm dizzy and weak and nauseous. I go to my knees on the grass, my forehead against the soft green blades. There's no reason to be acting like this. I'm in the heart of suburbia. I'm the safest I've been in years, but suddenly it's all coming crashing down around me.

Somewhere in the midst of near catatonic panic, strong arms scoop me up, carry me inside. I don't have the energy to resist. Tom takes me to the bedroom and lies me down on the little bed, covering me with an extra blanket or two, nice heavy weight over my shivering form.

"You're really in a bad way, hmmm," he murmurs softly. "Just keep breathing."

He sits beside me, this man who is a near total stranger and he rubs my back until the panic passes and I feel the natural calm that follows. It takes quite a long time to settle, but eventually I do, and then I feel silly, being stuck under all these blankets like a cowering child.

"Better?"

I nod.

"I'm going to get you some hot chocolate," he says. "You stay there."

What else can I do, but huddle beneath the blankets and wait for him to take care of me. I hate how I feel. I'm so weak, so pathetic. At least in Afghanistan I could feel brave.

Tom brings me the warm drink, helps me sit up and gives it to me.

"There you go."

"I'm so sorry," I say softly. "I'm so much trouble."

"You're fresh out of a war zone," he says. "You're not trouble."

I sip the chocolate. It's warm and its rich and it does what it's supposed to do - it makes me feel better. Now that I'm calmer, I can start to think again. That sucks, because all the thoughts are bad.

"I miss him," I admit.

"He misses you too," Tom says gently. "He wasn't happy about this, you know, but he thought I might be able to help."

"Yeah, you, a doctor."

"I never had anyone react so badly to me being a doctor before," he says with a handsome smirk. "It's usually a draw."

Obviously Ken didn't say anything about what happened to me in Chile. He kept my secret. That means something. I don't know what exactly, but something.

"Well, I'm weird and fucked up," I tell him. "And your brother really saddled you with some messed up stuff, so I'll go tomorrow."

"Nope. You'll stay right here."

"I really don't need another Ares man telling me what to do," I say wearily. I don't have the energy to fight him.

"I'm not trying to tell you what to do," he says. "I'm just trying to give you some space to be. I can handle anything you throw at me."

He's dead wrong about that.

"You were in the military too, weren't you?" I ask suddenly. I'm getting the strong feeling that he's not a general practitioner, and he has more in common with Ken than just genetics. He shares values and bearing.

"I was," he says. "Been out five years."

He's looking at me with a gaze which tells me he understands some things about me. Not everything. But maybe enough. I'm curious as to why he left, but that's not a question you ask someone you barely know.

"Get some rest," he says. "We'll deal with the rest of this in the morning."

"Alright," I concede. "Thanks."

He leaves me sitting in the bed that isn't mine, swaddled in blankets that aren't mine, sipping a fast cooling cup of hot chocolate and starting to feel just a little bit as if things might be alright after all.

KEN

"How is she?"

Mary cut me off, and I am not happy about that, but Tom's just got back to me, and he seems to have handled the situation, just like I knew he would.

"Upset, stressed, tired. She's going to be fine, I think."

"Keep a close eye on her. She's been through more than most."

"More than most?" He raises a brow. "She was just an embed, wasn't she? How much could she have been through?"

"There was more, before. She'll tell you when she's ready."

"Something medical, I'm guessing by the way she freaked when she found that I'm a doctor."

He's already starting to figure her out. Good.

I had several reasons to send her to Tom. First, and most simply, I want her looked after. Secondly, I know he needs someone to look after. Thirdly, I'm aware that in my line of work, I may not get to see her again. Ever.

As much as I want to, as much as I need to, things are not going well out here. The fighting is intensifying and our intelligence is sparse. The rest of my unit has joined me though, and that's something. There's dozens of us now, but there's still thousands of them.

Retreat would be the safe option, but it has not been authorized. We've been ordered to stay, to push through, and we will do what we're told even if, in the end, it means we don't go home again.

I want her safe. I want her with someone. And I want that someone to be Tom. He's the only man I know capable of handling someone like Mary. I'm scared for what will happen to her if I'm not around. The girl has an aura of tragedy about her. She needs someone to keep her in one piece - or at least stitch her up when she needs it. He will be that man.

"Look after her, Tom." That's all I can really say. She'll never forgive me if I tell him about the hospital. It's her story to tell, and I intend to let her tell it.

"Look after yourself, Ken," he says. "And don't worry about her. I've got her under control."

"That's what I thought," he smirks. "Seriously Tom, keep close tabs. And talk to her. She needs to talk."

TOM

"About what?"

Before Ken can avoid answering the question, I hear a siren sound through the speakers. He has to go. There's not even time for a goodbye as he rushes from his laptop, leaves it streaming as he slams out the door. Shit. I hate what he does, but I love him for doing it.

Suddenly, the house is quiet, but I'm no longer alone in it. Forty-two hours ago I was a single divorcee with nothing on the horizon. Now I have a spare bedroom full of trouble and a brother who needs my help.

Sitting back in my chair, I take stock of the situation. Mary is cute, and she's got the kind of temper which makes it obvious to me as to why Ken loves her. He always loved a challenge. So did I, until that challenge decided she loved a yoga instructor named Marque more.

I've been disillusioned with love for a long time. Medicine too. I've been on a hiatus for a few months, and intend to be on one for a few months more.

Now I have something to do, someone to look after. I can already tell this is going to be about more than just having a house guest. Mary needs more than a roof and access to the refrigerator. From what Ken's told me about her, and what I've already gathered for myself, she's a girl in need of some serious direction, discipline, and care.

I wasn't planning on seeking more female company. Certainly not eighteen years younger than me. She's actually young enough to be my daughter.

I close the laptop and go down to check on her. She's fast asleep by the looks of things. Walking in quietly, I take the remnants of the cup of hot chocolate out of her hands where it's still resting. Didn't even manage to put it on the nightstand before she fell asleep. She must be utterly exhausted, poor thing. Even in her sleep, I can see the way she juts her chin out defiantly at the world. She's proud. She's brave. But she's also small and hurt. I definitely have my work cut out for me with this little girl.

7

MARY

It's been a very long time since I woke up somewhere comfortable. When I open my eyes I find myself in a deep pile of blankets and coverlets. There is warm sun filtering through the window. Birds are singing outside. I'm home.

Well, in *a* home, anyway.

It feels like a lifetime since I woke up in a place like this. In a lot of ways, it literally was. I think the last time I woke up feeling this way, I was probably in my early teens.

After lying there for a while, orienting myself to the world, I get out of bed and go to the kitchen. Some things are habit. Even in strange new places where you don't really know the way you can still follow the smell.

Tom is up already, and cooking. The clock on the

wall says it's 10.00 am. I must have slept for half a day at least. I do feel a bit better for it though.

"Hey."

Seeing Tom makes me happy and gives me heartache at the same time. I miss Ken.

"Good morning, young lady," he says. "I made pancakes."

The *young lady* makes me think I'm in trouble. Then I remember that I don't get in trouble anymore. I left the man who can tell me I'm in trouble behind in Afghanistan.

I sit down and consume the pancakes, trying not to check Tom out too much. Today he's wearing a white shirt, sleeves rolled up, brown slacks. His hair is slightly damp from the shower, curling more than ever. Gives him a roguish appearance as he flips the last few pancakes, the muscles in his forearm rippling with the motions of spatula and pan.

The pancakes are really good. He knows how to make them light enough to absorb just the right amount of syrup. And there's hot chocolate too, not coffee. It's all really good and comforting and I'm almost starting to believe it's real.

Except, it can't be real. I can't possibly be here safe and sound, eating pancakes when there's people back in the desert. Where Ken is. Getting shot at. Wearing the smell of death.

The memory almost makes me gag. I put my fork down and push the plate away.

"Not hungry?" Tom's brow lifts the same damn way Ken's does.

"I've had enough, thank you. It was nice."

I'm trying to be as polite as I can, even as the dark thoughts come rushing in. I don't deserve this place. This comfort. I don't deserve these pancakes. I don't deserve a damn thing.

"What's on your mind?"

He asks the question gently. I don't want to answer it. He doesn't need to know. Better he doesn't.

"Mary," he says, his voice going a little deeper. "You were happy at first. What happened?"

"I remembered."

"What did you remember?"

"Everything."

"Ah," he nods. "Okay. Well. You and I need to have a conversation."

I don't want to have any conversations. I want to run. Really far. So far nobody can find me.

"Thanks for the pancakes," I say. "I'm going to get my things and go."

"Why?" He looks genuinely confused, reminding me that he's a civilian.

"Because I don't want to be your problem," I sigh. "I was Ken's problem, and I made everything worse. I might even have gotten some people killed. Bad things happen to me. And worse things happen to people who get involved with me. So I'm going to go."

"Some bad things might happen to you, sure," he counters. "And some bad things might happen to other people, but that doesn't mean you're the cause. And I'm not afraid of what might happen."

"That's because you don't know what's happened to me. You don't know where I've been, or who I've been involved with. Not even Ken knows. I went through some stuff. And then I went through some more stuff, and then I ran into Ken. And he sent me here. If you can think of a bad place or a bad person, I promise you I've been there and I've met them. Nobody really knows who I am, Tom. Not even Ken. Especially not Ken."

I'm being more honest than I've ever been with anyone. Tom's eyes never leave mine. He's listening. Intently listening. And he doesn't seem to be afraid, even though he really should be. Because Ken wasn't saving me from the dangers of Afghanistan when he sent me away. He was just exporting the danger. Right into this cozy little haven, where I know I don't belong, and into the life of this man who I can already tell is too good for me.

"There's a lot I don't know," he agrees when I stop talking. "Maybe you'll tell me some of it sometime. But that doesn't mean you need to leave. And it doesn't mean I'll let you." He says the last part with a smile, leaning casually on the counter. His words could be interpreted as threatening, if it weren't for his demeanor.

"I was safer in Afghanistan. That's the truth," I say. "I got out of… the place I was in, and then I went and did some things with some people. I owe money. I owe blood. I was a very bad girl, Tom. In ways you don't understand."

TOM

This little girl has a flair for the dramatic. Maybe she's trying to warn me. Or maybe this is just a very dramatic way for a small woman to make herself look bigger. Physically, she's on the smaller side. And I know from Ken and from her that she's a journalist. It's really hard to believe that she poses anyone any danger at all.

Regardless, I listen.

"So you're afraid people will come looking for you here?"

"I'm afraid that I have some heavy karma coming my way, and I don't want more people involved than have to be."

"Well, I'll deal with that as and when it happens."

"You're not equipped to deal with anything," she smirks.

I feel my palms tingle. If you ask me, this girl is begging for a spanking. A good, long, over the knee butt warming. That would settle her down nicely. But she's my brother's lover. And my guest. And I don't spank girls who don't ask for it very, very nicely.

———

Seven days later...

"Mary!"

"What?"

"Can you put your wrappers in the trash, please?"

"Huh? Oh yeah. Sure," she says, going right back to watching the television, turning the volume up to drown out the vacuum which I'm pushing around the room in a futile attempt to get my place looking like something other than a bomb site.

Ken didn't send her here to laze around and mess up my house. He sent her here to keep her out of trouble. She's not technically in trouble - not with anyone but me, that is.

It's quickly apparent that Mary does whatever Mary wants, whenever Mary wants. The hours she keeps are atrocious. She's up until the small hours of the morning and I'm sure I haven't seen her up before midday any day this week.

She refuses to talk to Ken, which works out because Ken's more busy and less available than he has ever been. That area of the world is hot as hell right now. I'm worried for him, to be honest. I've been worried about him since he was born though. Perpetual big brother, that's me.

"Can you move your legs, please?"

"Huh?"

"Can you move your legs?" I raise my voice over vacuum and television, feeling like I'm picking up after a rebellious teenage daughter.

"Do I need to assign you chores, little girl?"

She smirks and rolls her eyes. "You want me to clean? I'll clean."

"Yes, I want you to clean."

"Okay. No problem. I'll do it later."

"You'll do it now."

She looks up from her computer with an impressive scowl on her pretty face. "I'm busy now."

"Busy doing what?"

"None of your business." She closes the laptop.

I get the impression she's testing me. Or maybe punishing me. For looking like Ken. But I'm not Ken, I and deal with problems differently.

"Mary, you're very welcome here," I say. "But you're going to have to start helping out too. You're a grown woman. You know better than to leave a mess around for someone else to clean up."

"You know what," she says, taking immediate offense. "You're condescending as hell."

God this girl needs a spanking. A really good, long, hard spanking. Pants down for sure. Maybe not on the bare, but definitely over her underwear. It's not even a sexual thing. She needs bringing in line. Badly. But it's not my place. Ken is going to have his work cut out for him when he gets back. In the meantime, I guess I'm going to be vacuuming twice a day.

MARY

He looks so much like Ken when he's irritated. I

know I shouldn't be giving him trouble. Hell, the mess even irritates me. It takes effort to leave wrappers everywhere. If he doesn't give me what I want soon, I'm going to leave the milk out. I've seen the way his eye twitches at the milk rings left from coffee. He'd probably totally self-combust if I left the milk out overnight.

This is definitely immature on my part, but I'm mad, and I can't take my anger out on the man who deserves it. I'm not even taking it out on Tom. I'm just… letting it leak a bit.

Truth is, I miss having someone keep me in line. It was only a week with Ken, but knowing I couldn't get away with my usual shit actually felt really good. I feel like he got me addicted to him and then sent me away. And now I'm lost. Sitting in this comfortable house with this guy who is way too nice for his own good, and wondering just how far I can push him.

"You want me to clean? I'll clean."

I pick up a foil wrapper from a protein bar which was sitting on the couch next to me, look him dead in the eye, and drop it on the ground.

He lets out a sigh. "Little girl, do you want a spanking? Is that it?"

"No!" My denial is hot, and swift, and a total lie.

"Then quit being a brat," he says, bending to pick the wrapper up.

I feel a mix of disappointment and guilt. Guilt for being an asshole to this guy. Disappointment because I didn't get what I wanted. What the hell am I doing?

Tom's giving me a place to stay and he's a really cool guy and I am being a total dick about all of this.

"I'm sorry," I say, pushing off the couch. "I'll help tidy."

"Thanks," he says with what seems to be a genuine smile. We both get down to tidying and soon the place is spotless.

"Good job," he says, holding his hand up for a high five.

He doesn't seem to hold my behavior against me. Nice. Far too nice. I reach up and slap his hand.

"Gimme another," he jokes, lifting his hand higher still. So high I have to jump for it. It's a goofy thing to want, but I can't leave the guy hanging, so I give a little jump. As I rise into the air, my shirt comes up, exposing my stomach a little. No big deal, except I see his eyes dip, and then widen. The scars. He's seen the fucking scars.

It's enough to make me try to abort the act mid-air, which isn't possible according to our laws of gravity, so instead of slapping his hand, I end up clumsily falling almost into him. Tom catches me and steadies me on my feet.

"You okay?"

"Fine." I brush his hands away. "I'm fine. Thanks."

Forcing a smile, I grab my laptop and retreat quickly to the bedroom.

TOM

A fear of doctors, and a body which looks like it's been operated on heavily. Has she been sick at some point in her life? Maybe needed some exploratory surgery? I only got a quick glimpse, but there were an awful lot of scars on that girl's midsection and something about them just felt plain wrong.

It's not my business. She's just crashing at my place, I tell myself.

But my feet are carrying me to her room. And my knuckles are tapping on the door. And now I'm opening it.

"Go away!"

She's been crying. I can hear it in her voice.

"Mary?" I say her name softly.

"What?"

"Are you okay, Mary?"

"I'm great," she lies.

I don't know how to have the conversation with her, but Ken told me she needed to talk, and I agree.

"I don't want to pry…"

"Then don't," she snaps. She's prickly and I don't blame her. She sits on the bed, her knees up to her chest, her arms wrapped around them. She's defending herself against the world. Against me.

My heart goes out to her. I can sense that she needs help, but she doesn't know how to take it, or how to ask for it. Ken wanted me to talk to her. It's time I did.

"Little girl." The words escape my mouth before I can stop them. I've been refraining from calling her that as much as possible, even though it's been on the tip of my tongue since we met. "I think you and I should talk."

"About what?"

"Well, maybe about some of the trouble you're in."

"No," she snorts. "No thank you. And I don't want to talk about your brother either."

"Okay well. What about..." I trail off. The scars. I want to know how she got them. Actually, I'd like to examine them. But I know she won't allow that and I can't force it.

"You're a nice guy," she says flatly. "But you're out of your depth with me, okay, Tom?"

That makes me smile. "Why would I be out of my depth with you?"

"Because you just are. I know you saw those scars. You're curious. No, I didn't to them to myself."

"Of course not. They're obviously surgical."

"Yeah."

"Were you sick?"

"Nope."

The tone in her voice is changing, and so is the look in her eye. It's as if she's slipping away from me even as she's sitting right there in front of me. It's almost eerie.

"Mary."

"What?" She snaps back into the room.

I have more than enough medical training to recognize dissociation when I see it. This girl has been through serious trauma of one kind or another.

"You can talk to me," I say gently.

"I know. I speak English."

"I mean, you can really talk to me. I keep secrets. And I don't judge."

"Then you're an idiot," she says. "You should judge."

"I won't judge you."

"Yes you will," she smirks at me. "You just think you won't because you can't imagine me as being anything other than a little victim for you to rescue. Just like your brother. I was too much trouble for him, and I'll be too much trouble for you too."

"You weren't too much trouble for him. He wanted you safe. And you're not too much trouble for me."

"Just leave me alone," she sighs.

"Mary," I say, letting my tone get sharper. "I'm getting a little tired of the attitude."

I have her attention now. I can practically see her ears prick up at the injection of sternness into my voice. She needs to be looked after. She wants to be looked after too, I think. But she won't let it happen unless I show her I'm in control.

"What are you going to do about it?"

I'm sure she intends the question to be rebellious, but I can hear the hope in her voice.

"Well, for starters, you're going to lose privileges if you keep acting up."

"You're not my dad," she laughs. "You can't take away my privileges."

"You're under my roof, young lady. And while you are, you will obey my rules or face the consequences."

"Like what?" She's giggling now, and her cheeks are pink with what I'm sure isn't amusement.

"Like an early curfew and bed time. Like no dessert. Like limited electronics time."

"Okay seriously, Tom, you're not my dad."

I fix her with a long, stern look. "Yes, I am little girl. As long as you're here, consider me your daddy."

She's not laughing anymore. She's blushing. The look in her eye isn't defiant anymore. It's soft. She lowers her gaze, her fingers playing with the blanket. When she speaks, her voice is softer and lighter than I've heard it before.

"Okay."

MARY

I've been drowning since I left Afghanistan. Trying to keep myself together. Trying to manage the oceans of emotions which threaten to overwhelm me regularly.

I need something. I need someone. Right now, Tom is all I have and it feels like he just threw me a lifeline when he offered to be my daddy. I never had a daddy. My father died before I was old enough to really remember him. I don't even know what it means to have a daddy. But when those words came out of his mouth, they felt right. Tom already feels like family.

I love Ken. I lust for him. Tom is handsome as hell, but I don't feel the same way about him as I do Ken. Monogamy in action, I guess. Or maybe it's just that Ken is utterly ruthless and unyielding and would probably have whipped my ass on day one if I'd tried any of the shit on him which I just tried on Tom.

"Good," he smiles warmly. "Then that's settled. No more of the attitude, no more of the messes, no more of the rudeness. Just you and me, getting along."

I snort a little. He has to know that's not the end of it.

"Well, it's a start," he says. "Mary…"

"What?"

"I'd like to examine those scars."

I shake my head. "Sorry, no."

"I'm guessing you got them under some adverse circumstances, and from how you reacted when you found out I'm a doctor, I'm guessing you haven't seen one for a while."

My palms are sweating. My mouth and throat are getting dry.

"No," I croak.

"Okay," he holds up his big hands in surrender. "Not going to force anything."

"Good."

"Let's just talk," he suggests.

I don't want to talk. He's seen the scars and now he feels sorry for me, and though he's being sweet to me that makes me mad. I fucking hate it when this happens.

"I'm not weak, and I don't need to be taken care of."

"True and false," he says. "You absolutely need to be taken care of. You've spent a week proving that to both of us. And besides, even if you didn't need it, I'd do it anyway because I promised Ken I would."

"You can't give me what I need," I say, immediately wishing I hadn't. I need to stop this conversation. It's getting way too real.

"Not all of what you need," he agrees. "Because you need Ken. But I can keep you in line well enough until he gets back."

"Can you?"

He smiles. "Mhm."

I try not to visibly squirm, wondering if he means what I mean. I need a spanking. God. That's weird to admit even to myself. I just want so badly to be able to let go, to feel like someone else has me under control. I wish Tom would spank me. I want my bottom to hurt. I want to cry. I want to forget who I and where I am and why I'm here and just be free of the burden of existence for a bit.

"But you have to ask for it," he adds, unexpectedly.

"What?"

"You have to ask for what you need. Use your big girl words."

"I don't know what I need," I lie.

"Yes, you do. You've been trying to bait me into doing it all week."

I feel my face go flame red. He knew. The whole time, he knew exactly what I was doing. How fucking embarrassing.

"Sorry," I mumble, turning my face away from him. Jesus. I've humiliated myself and got nothing for it. I feel small and silly and utterly like a little girl who just got caught trying to lie to her dad.

"You can ask for a spanking."

I let out a little squeak as he says the word that has been floating through my head since I got here.

"No, I can't."

"Why not? Pride?"

"I guess."

"My little girl doesn't get to have much in the way of pride," he says, coming to sit on the edge of the bed. He reaches out and brushes his fingers through my hair gently. His touch is so kind and so gentle, I find myself leaning into it.

"Ask me for it," he murmurs gently.

I try to find the words.

"Please… sp…"

Spank is a fucking impossible word to say under pressure. I stutter and stammer my way through it so much it's basically incomprehensible. "

"Sp…pp..p.. ank me."

"And what do you call me?"

Oh shit. He's going to make me call him…

I curl up on myself and hide my face, but Tom gently guides my chin back toward him. "Ask me for it, little girl. Ask me nicely."

"Please, spank me… daddy…" I practically whisper the last part of the word, but it's enough.

"Alright, little girl. I'll spank you."

And he does.

He takes me by the arm and slowly guides me over

his lap. I relax and let it happen. I let this man, who is so kind and so strong, take me right over his thighs. We're so close right now. His hard leg is beneath my hips, his strong arm is wrapped around my waist.

This feels nothing like when Ken spanked me. When he punished me it was passion and fire and pure hard dominance. Tom cradles me and when his palm meets my ass, it's with a stroke which is firm and hard enough to make it sting, but it doesn't ignite the same fire.

And that's a good thing. Because it's means I'm safe. He's safe. Tom holds me and he spanks me, his big hand peppering the seat of my jeans with firm slaps which sink through me, sending wave after wave of security through my body.

"You can be a good girl," he says, lecturing me in the kindest way you can be lectured. "And you're going to be a good girl from here on out, aren't you, Mary?"

"I'll try," I gasp.

His palm finds my ass a little harder, intensifying the heat and the sting.

"And every time you start to feel lost or afraid or alone, you're going to come to me," he says. "And I'm going to do this for you."

The spanking isn't hard enough to make me cry, but his promise is. The floodgates I've been holding closed spring open, and with them come tears. Tears I can't restrain in any way. I start sobbing over Tom's lap. He immediately picks me up and settles me on his knee, cuddling me close and letting me cry all over his shirt.

"There, there, little girl, he murmurs. "It's going to be okay."

I don't know if it is going to be okay. But it is going to be better than it was, I think. As he holds me, his arms loose about my waist in a comforting, paternal grip, I start to settle down.

"One more thing,"

"What?"

He brushes a stray tear away with his thumb.

"You're going to talk to Ken again."

TOM

"Well fuck you, Ken!"

Their conversation is not going well. It's not surprising. They both need one another and they can't have one another. Ken is too much of a hard ass to show her how fucking exhausted he is from being over there, and Mary is too much of a brat to see that he loves her with everything he has. They talk past each other regularly. It's strange how two people who have so much in common, who are basically made for one another, somehow manage to disagree almost all the time.

She wouldn't be acting out like this if he were here, that's for sure. I hear him growl something to that effect.

"Well, whatever," she snaps. "You're never coming back anyway."

"I will be there next week," Ken snarls from the laptop. "And then your ass is mine."

"Next week?" Her tantrum stops mid-stride.

"Yes," he says, his expression still stony. "Seven days. So get in all the sitting time you can, Mary, because when I get there…"

"Next week!"

"Mhm."

I hear him start to smile through his voice.

"Oh my god!" Her voice gets all high pitched and squeaky. "Next week!"

She comes running in to grab me. "Tom, Ken is going to be here next week!"

"So I heard," I smile as she throws herself at me in a hug.

"Next week!"

MARY

Fresh from the shower, I look at myself in the mirror. It has been a long time since I let myself see what I look like. Usually I avoid looking into the glass until I'm dressed. Then I don't have to see what they took. I don't have to see what I've become.

Today I stand and I force myself to look, because soon he will be looking again. I want to see what he sees. Maybe it's not so bad…

…

… It's even worse than I remembered.

I am trammeled with marks. Lines. Scars. I am

geometric where I should be smooth. My skin puckers where it should lay flat.

How could Ken look at me and see anything worthy? Let alone a woman he wants to have sex with?

He will be back soon. I will have to face him again. The man I bait through the computer will be made flesh in front of me and he will have his way with me. He's told me so enough times that I believe him.

I wrap my arms over my breasts, hide the missing nipple. Sometimes I wonder what they did with it. Tiny frisbee?

I snort at my dark thought. It's not funny, but it helps me deal.

———

A tap at the door makes me yank a towel around my naked body as Tom's voice comes from the other side.

"You okay in there, Mary?"

I roll my eyes at the mirror. What is he, psychic?

"Why wouldn't I be?"

"Just checking."

He might actually be a bit psychic. Not in any kind of paranormal way though. Tom just has a sense of empathy so strong he seems to catch my feelings almost before I have them.

"I'm fine."

"Your breakfast is getting cold."

That's my cue to stop dredging up the darkness and get some clothes on.

I get dressed and go and sit at the kitchen counter, where Tom has made a breakfast spread that would make a hotel chef cry. Croissants. Juices. Cheeses. Grapes. Three different kinds of jam.

"What's this for?"

"Just felt like spoiling my little girl," he says with a flicker of a wink.

"You're way too fucking nice, Tom."

"I'm just the right amount of nice, and no swearing, please."

He really does treat me like I'm his kid. It's kind of weird in a way, but it's also really fucking sweet.

As I pick at what is enough breakfast for a small army, he makes conversation.

"You looking forward to Ken coming home?"

"Of course."

"So you've forgiven him for sending you here?"

"Yeah," I shrug. "I mean. I get it. He had to do what he had to do."

Tom smiles. "You've come a really long way."

"Yeah, from Afghanistan."

"No, brat," he snorts. "I mean, when you got here you were so angry. I could barely talk to you. But you seem happier now. Settled."

"I'd like to be settled," I mumble through crumbs.

"You can stay here as long as you like or need…"

"… or until Ken says otherwise," I smirk.

"Or that," Tom agrees. He doesn't look happy about that. I think he likes having me here. I'm company. Not good company necessarily, but company.

"So what's your story, doc?"

"What do you mean?"

"Why aren't you working?"

"It pays to take some time off every now and then," he says, turning his attention to cleaning crumbs off the counter. "Like when your marriage falls apart."

I don't want to pry, but I can see Tom being thrown off kilter by something like a marriage breakup. He's strong, but sensitive, and he wears it on his sleeve.

"How long have you been off work?"

"I'll be getting back to the hospital in a couple of months," he says. "Don't worry about me, little girl. I'm just enjoying my time off now. The wallowing is over."

Maybe it is. Maybe it isn't.

I know better than anyone that some things can hurt for a very, very long time.

———

Later that day, I'm watching television. Tom has gone out for groceries and I'm just relaxing when I hear the doorbell. It's not a common sound, and at first I don't even recognize it. It rings several times more in very quick succession though, and I soon realize that there's an uptight brunette standing at the door with a screwed up expression like a dog just pissed on her.

I open the door. "Yeah?"

"Where is Thomas?"

"Thomas?"

"Typical," she mutters under her breath. "His bimbos never know his name."

Bimbo? Did she just call me a fucking bimbo?

"Doctor. Ares," she says in a loud, slow voice. "Is. he. in?"

I fold my arms over my chest. I don't like this woman. I don't like her tone. I don't like her face. I don't like her shoes. I don't like anything about her.

"Who's asking?"

"His wife," she says haughtily.

"You mean ex-wife?"

The woman bristles and looks me over with open hostility. "So you're what he replaced me with."

"No," I say, speaking before I can think. "He replaced you with a cock-sleeve full of wasps. He says fucking it reminds him of you."

Her expression is priceless. Her jaw drops and she makes a spluttering sound which indicates she has no comeback whatsoever.

"Mary, go to your room!"

Turns out, Tom is home after all. He must have come through the back door with the groceries. Now he's standing behind me, looking about as unhappy as I've ever seen him look.

This isn't my fight. I shouldn't get involved. So I don't. I lift my hands up and walk away - as far as the hall corner where I can still see and hear what's going on beyond.

"You still have that sick fetish of ordering women

around," she says, her voice loud enough for the neighbors to hear. What a bitch.

"Is there a problem, Stephanie?" Tom says, remaining impressively calm.

"Yes, there's a problem. I need an advance on my alimony. I'm going out of state with Hector."

"I can't do that," Tom says. "You'll get your alimony at the usual time."

"I want my alimony," she says, her tone getting nastier. "Or…"

"Or what?" He lowers his voice a little. "You've already gotten me suspended pending an investigation. You've already taken the apartment in the city, and the car. What else do you want?"

"You're obliged to keep me in the style I became accustomed to."

My blood boils as I listen to this bullshit. Tom is the sweetest guy on Earth and this woman is trying to shake him down. There's threat in her tone, like she has something on him she plans to use to try to ruin his life if he doesn't do as she says.

I go to the bathroom to grab something, and then I come back. When I do, she's still outside, trying to badger Tom into giving her more money. Fuck everything about this.

"I'm sorry," I say sweetly, pushing past him. "Tom doesn't have any money right now. He spent it all on this stupid spoiled whore repellent."

I have a can of toilet spray air freshener. It's the only thing for pieces of shit like her. I spray it in her direction, a nice thick mist. She starts making coughing sounds and waving her hands about, but that's not the worst of what I have planned for her if she doesn't get the fuck off his porch.

"Go away, bitch," I hiss. "We already gave to the gold-digging slut-athon."

She opens her mouth to speak, but gags on the scent of concentrated lavender and wild flowers.

Fortunately for her, Tom sees what I have in the other hand and grabs it off me before I can use the lighter which would have turned the smelly spray into a ball of fire.

He slams the door shut in her face, more for her protection than anything. Through the glass, I see her rushing back to her car as fast as her high heels will take her.

I look at Tom, expecting to see him smile. Instead, he rounds on me, his face a mask of stern anger.

"You do NOT use home-made flame throwers on my ex-wife."

"Not when you take the lighter off me, I don't," I say. "I was trying to help."

"Help? By burning her?"

"I was only going to do that if she didn't leave."

"You don't do that at ALL!" He thunders at me. "What's wrong with you?"

It's my turn to stand, stunned. He's actually yelling at me, after I tried to defend him.

Tears spring to my eyes. That last part of the question is like a knife to my stomach. What's wrong with me? Fucking everything apparently.

"I'm sorry, I guess I should marry some guy and ruin his fucking life. That would be normal. There wouldn't be anything wrong with me then, would there!?"

TOM

She turns and runs away from me, tears streaming down her face.

Shit.

Stephanie drives me crazy. Always has done. And what Mary just did was so wrong. There's no question about that. She has to know better than that, though I'm somewhat afraid that she doesn't. I think I just saw why Ken threw her out of Afghanistan.

She is sobbing on her bed when I find her, crying real tears which make her shoulders shake. I could take a hairbrush to her butt for half an hour and not end up making her this miserable.

"Mary…"

"Go away."

I sit down next to her on the bed and put my hand on her shoulder. She predictably flinches away. I put it back on her back, nice and low, and firm enough to hold her in place. She squirms a bit, but accepts it after a second or two.

"I'm not normal," she growls into the bed.

Ken was right. This girl is a handful. She doesn't

respond to things the way most people do. She's hyper-defensive, and overly aggressive in a way that's frankly confusing. Most of the time she seems 'normal', whatever that is. But every now and then, she'll do something so far out of the realm of normality it makes me wonder what on earth she's been through.

"Who taught you to act that way?"

"Doesn't matter," she mumbles.

"It absolutely does."

"Everybody knows about aerosols and fire," she shrugs.

True. But not everybody tries to use them on annoying ex-wives. Mary could have done Stephanie serious harm. Criminal harm. There's so much anger in this girl I'm looking after, a dangerous amount.

"Now you know what I'm really like, huh? I told you Ken didn't do you any favors when he sent me here."

"I'm sorry I said the thing about being normal," I apologize. "Stephanie makes me... well, I lose my cool around her."

"So do I," Mary mutters into the bedding.

"Apparently so," I agree. "But you know that was wrong, right?"

"She was trying to extort you for money. I shoulda cut her fingers off," Mary growls fiercely.

"Okay, well, no..."

"Yes. That's why she does what she does. Because people like her can do whatever they want, and people like me..."

She bursts into incoherent tears again. All I can do is rub her back and try to settle her down.

"I know you were trying to help," I soothe. "I know you were just trying to defend me. But I don't need defending. Stephanie makes a lot of noise, but she doesn't get what she wants. It's why she left me in the first place. I wasn't enough of a pushover for her. You let me take care of you, okay, little girl?"

Mary rolls over to face me. Her face is streaked with misery, but she seems calmer.

"Don't tell Ken," she says. "He wouldn't like that."

"He would not," I agree.

Ken would whip her ass for what she just did. Hell, I should whip her ass for it, but I don't have the heart. As misguided as she was, that was her way of helping. I need to make sure she doesn't feel compelled to 'help' again.

The silver lining to all this is that Ken will be home soon. If there's anyone on the planet who can deal with someone like Mary, it's him.

8

MARY

Ken is coming home today. I've been waiting for this day for what feels like forever. It feels like a hundred Christmases and Birthdays all rolled up into one, and I'm so excited I didn't sleep at all last night, or maybe even the night before that.

He's coming home. We're going to be together. I'm going to make all my shitty behavior up to him. There are a few dark thoughts associated with that, but I push them away. I'm happy, just genuinely completely happy and I won't let anything get in my way.

"Hey Tom," I say as he comes out for breakfast. I've made waffles and pancakes and toast. Carb loading for happiness.

The moment I see his face, I know there's something wrong. He looks serious, and he never looks serious.

"What's wrong?"

"I've got some news," Tom says. "Ken's still coming home, but he says it could be a few more days. He's been held up."

"Held up with what?" I try not to show how my eyes fill with tears almost immediately, but of course that doesn't fool Tom one little bit. He can read me like a book. Half the time he knows what I'm going to do before I know.

"I'm not sure, but he said it's nothing to worry about. Just procedure or something."

"He said today!"

"It's going to be a little longer."

"He said a week! That's today. It's supposed to be today!"

I'm on the verge of a hysterical meltdown. I was holding on to this date more tightly than I knew. I have been tolerating civilian life, allowing myself to slide into the comfortable numbness of advertisements with talking toilet paper, just occasionally sparking into what feels like real life when I'm in trouble with Tom.

Trying to keep control of my emotions, I curl my hands on the counter. I feel something sharp, but don't register it as pain until Tom exclaims.

"Mary!"

"Fuck!"

I've grabbed a knife by the pointy end and cut through my hand like a goddamn idiot.

"Easy," Tom soothes, picking up my hand and

raising it above my chest height. "Oh okay, yes little girl, this is quite nasty. You're going to need stitches."

I stare at him blankly. "Stitches?"

"Come on I'll take you to the hospital."

The very mention of a hospital throws my already over adrenalized system into total chaos. "No! No hospitals!"

"You need to go. Now come on."

I lash out wildly, frightened beyond belief. Blood goes everywhere as I fight him with every bit of strength I have, thrashing and clawing around as he drags me out of the kitchen and away from the sharp and hot things.

"Okay settle down," he says, holding me hard against his body. He and the walls are now both smeared in sanguine red traces of my essence. "It's going to have to be sutured, Mary, it's too deep."

"So suture it. You're a doctor."

"I don't have local anesthetics here."

"So do it without."

"Little girl, I am not…"

"Do. It. Without."

TOM

I have seen small flashes of this side of her, the side with is simultaneously terribly afraid and brave beyond belief. That wound is going to need at least four stitches, and I want her numb, but I don't have the injectables at home. This is ridiculous. If I were practicing at a clinic, I'd run her in there, but I'm not right now so she needs to go to the ER.

I wrap a tight bandage around the wound and sit her down on a stool. "Don't move."

She sits there like a statue as I go and get myself ready for what might be the fight of my life. To my relief, she hasn't run off by the time I get back. She doesn't look like she's moved so much as a muscle, actually. There's something more than a little eerie about it.

I offer her a pill. "Okay, take this."

"What is it?"

"Codeine. It will take the edge off."

"No thank you."

I suspect she knows the pill in my hand isn't codeine. It's actually a sedative. She needs proper medical attention. I can't sew her up here in the kitchen. I could make her take it, I suppose. I could grab her and force her to go to the hospital, call an ambulance with paramedics who will sedate her for me. The options run through my mind, but I know they're all forms of betrayal she will not tolerate. If I force this now, I will lose her, maybe forever.

Hell. I'm going to have to do this as she's asked me to. Without anesthetic. It's going to be a mess I know, as soon as she feels the needle, she's probably going to panic and cause more damage to herself and the property. Sometimes, dealing with this girl is like having a wild animal in the house.

"Okay," I say, unwinding the bandage. "I'm going to

give this a clean over the sink and then we're going to do this. It's going to hurt."

"It's okay."

I know how she yelps when I paddle her butt. I know this isn't going to be okay. But we really don't have a choice right now.

She manages to hold still as I wash the wound out with saline and I start to think maybe this might work. She is pale though, so I make sure she stays propped against me in case she passes out. Don't need a head injury as well as a gash to treat.

"Okay, now this is going to hurt, but try your best to keep still," I say as I begin to suture her wound.

Mary holds perfectly still as the needle threads through her flesh. It's almost frightening how in control of the pain she appears to be, but the look in her eyes tells me it's not control. It's dissociation. Someone… or rather, a whole lot of someones over an extended period of time taught her how to separate herself from pain.

Jesus. This poor girl. She told me she had been hurt and damaged, but I never truly understood until right now. With her sitting in my kitchen, barely blinking as I weave her hand back together.

"Good girl," I soothe as I apply a last bandage. "All done."

"All done?" She looks at me, and it is the most eerie thing, to see her return to her eyes, as if she just stepped out of her body for a bit.

"All done," I confirm.

"Thank you," she nods.

I tidy up the medical supplies, getting them out of her way. She sits there quietly, sadly, watching me.

"You see now, don't you," she says in a soft voice.

"What's that, little girl?"

"You see how broken I am."

I look over at her. "You're not broken. I just sewed you up."

"Yes I am," she says without so much as a hint of a smile. "I'm cracked right down the middle."

"You had some serious trauma," I say, making sure everything is properly disposed of. "I don't think you're broken."

"You're either lying or stupid. Or maybe both."

There's a hollow quality to her words I don't like. I feel as though she's slipping away from me again, as if she's not really in the room anymore. That, I won't allow. She needs to stay present.

"That's enough!" I snap the words harshly enough to get her attention. Usually, being sweet to her works, but right now she needs to hear something harsher and more stern. "You will speak to me with respect, young lady. I know you have had some very difficult experiences…"

"Difficult experiences!" She laughs at me in tones devoid of humor. "They cut my fucking womb out."

At first, I'm sure I heard her wrong. Then I think she must be exaggerating.

"You mean you've had a hysterectomy?"

"I've had a fuck-you-ectomy," she says bitterly.

"Why?"

"Because that's what they did there. I saw them do it."

This doesn't sound right. People don't see their hysterectomies.

"Are you sure?"

"Yes, I'm fucking sure," she says, confession coming in the heat of the moment as she loses her temper. "They didn't like to put us completely under. Too much risk of death. And they liked to make us watch. They told me what they were doing. They pulled that organ out of me and they put it in a box, and they told me someone else would put it to good use. And that's not even the worst thing I saw them do."

She's shaking. I want to hug her, but I think touching her right now might set her off even worse than what she is. So I stand there, and I listen as she tells me the things I'm sure she hasn't told anybody before.

"What was the worst thing you saw them do?"

I don't want to hear it, not really, but I need to. She needs me to hear it. She needs to be able to bring this stuff to light and have it not destroy her world.

"After they took me, in between experiments. They used me as... they made me... assist in some things."

"What things?"

She's getting that faraway look in her eye again, and her voice is going flat, recounting something nobody should ever have to remember, let alone experience. Maybe I shouldn't have asked. But it's too late now.

"A woman tried to escape. She almost made it out. She was down in the normal wards, screaming about being a captive. But they caught her and they brought her back up, and they…" her eyes go dark and hollow. "You don't want to hear this."

"I do."

She looks at me, and before she even opens her mouth, I feel a chill in the air. Her eyes are a portal to the place she was held, and it's as if I can feel a small amount of what it was like to be there. The hair stands up on the back of my neck. My heart beats faster.

This girl who has been so much lively trouble is now still as a statue. The color seems to be sucked from around her and when she speaks, her voice has a tone to it which makes it hard to even recognize.

"They took out her liver."

I cough. "What?"

"Just to see what would happen."

She runs her undamaged fingers back and forth over the counter, as if trying to soothe herself. She looks out the window, then back at me.

"It took her three days to die."

"Jesus," I murmur, horrified and slightly confused. "I wouldn't have thought you could live more than an hour or two."

"Three days," she repeats. "They made me take notes. They made me watch to see what would happen if I ever tried to escape. If it wasn't for Ken… I would still be there. Missing more and more parts until…"

I wrap my arms around her as she cracks and starts

to cry. In an instant, she transforms from cold statue to broken woman. The tears flow in a torrent of pure misery and grief.

They took so much from her. They carved out the thing at the very core of her. They took her chance at motherhood and they stripped her faith in humanity away. There's no getting that back. Once you've seen things that depraved, you're forever changed no matter what happens afterward.

She needs to cry. I need to fucking kill someone, but I subdue my more vicious impulses to comfort her. It's hard. I don't know how to make this better - because it can't be made better. What they've taken from her can't ever be replaced.

I understand so much more about her now. And I know why Ken is so insistent she be safe. Mary deserves to be safe. She needs to be protected and cared for. She needs to be shown that the world still has softer sides. I've been doing all that basically on instinct, from the first moment I saw her standing in the airport looking lost and waif-like with that back-pack that damn near dwarfed her.

"Nothing like that is ever going to happen to you again," I promise her. "You're safe now. I've got you, okay, little girl, I've got you."

Her tears are more like the howls of a wounded animal. I am hearing the sound of pain repressed for months on end, bursting free from the dam she constructed to hold it back. Afghanistan would have kept her safe from it. In dangerous places, the mind naturally blocks the worst of trauma to keep the individual alive. But she's here now, in a suburban kitchen, and in her disappointment at missing Ken, her defenses have finally failed her.

All I can do is hold her through it all, carry her to the couch and let her curl up in a little ball in my lap and cry through the misery and the pain and the fear. It takes a very long time, and hearing all that coming from her sweet mouth is almost too much for me to handle. I want to go and tear the throats out of everybody who had a hand in hurting her, but she needs me right now, and she needs me to be warm and open and loving.

"Are you okay?"

She asks the question in a small voice, her face stained with tears as she peers up from under wet, dark hair to inquire after my well-being.

"I'm fine, little girl," I reassure her.

"You're not," she says. "You're angry. Like me."

"I am angry," I admit as I hold her close and try not to think murderous thoughts. "I wish I could do something to hurt those people."

"Ken hurt them," she says. "He hurt them badly."

"Oh I bet he did." I'm almost jealous that he got to do that. I want to hurt them too. I want to hurt anyone who ever hurt her.

"So now you know," she says. "Now you know all the things. More than anybody."

"I do," I agree. "And I still want you, little girl."

"Why?" Her voice cracks. "I'm broken."

"You might have been broken, but you're healing," I say. "That's why this hurts so much."

MARY

Am I healing? I didn't think I would ever heal from what happened to me. I don't feel like I'm healing. I feel raw and pathetic and so terribly broken I'm not worthy of his time, but Tom holds me and he tells me that it's going to get better, and there's a little part of me that believes him somehow. This man gives me hope.

"You really think I'm healing?"

"Mhm," he nods. "I do. Healing can hurt, Mary. Sometimes just as much as the original wound did. Sometimes more. But it happens. All you have to do is hold on. Can you do that?"

I nod. I don't have any choice. There were times in the hospital where I'm sure I could have died if I wanted to. I was weak enough that I could have slipped away. A lot of people did. But I stayed. I didn't know back then why I was staying, but I think I know why now. I stayed for this. For Ken. For Tom. For the chance at a life beyond those sterile walls.

This is a world I thought I'd never experience. This is something I knew I never deserved. Actually, it's something I know I don't deserve. This all has to end, and soon. But before it does, I'll bask in it and maybe that will get me through what inevitably happens next.

———

"Am I interrupting something?"

A voice at the door makes my heart leap. I stare at Tom, then look toward the front door, which is being opened as I stare. I can barely believe what my eyes are showing me.

A man is standing there. Tall. Powerful. Handsome as hell. I recognize him, but it takes a second for my brain to realize that he's really here.

It's Ken. It's fucking Ken!

I pull out of Tom's arms, and run to him, the few feet from the lounge to the front door feeling like the longest run I've ever done. "I thought you weren't coming today!" I throw myself into his arms and hold him so tight I can feel the hard muscles of his body contracting beneath my grasp.

He picks me up and holds me close. "I'm sorry," he says. "There was a mixup and…"

I don't even care. All I care about is the fact that it's him. He's here. He's safe. He's not being shot at for now at least and he's mine. He smells like him, a unique musk which is forever etched in my mind. I can feel my internal chemistry going crazy at recognizing it, an internal fizzing of excitement and immediate desire.

He kisses me, his hand at the back of my head, his fingers curled in my hair. Our tongues twirl with passion and need and the sheer relief of being reunited and tears of sheer joy begin to roll down my face. He's here. He's back. He came for me. He's mine.

Ken walks into the house, carrying me like a great

weight on his front and sits down on the couch next to Tom.

"Hey bro."

"Hey man."

They're no less pleased to see each other than I am to see him, I'm sure of that, but some men express feelings toward other men differently, in other words, by not really expressing them at all.

I draw back a little, just to look at him. I want to take his face in. I want to let my eyes feast on him. He looks a bit tired after a series of long flights, but he looks so fucking handsome too. I look at him, and he looks back.

"What have you been doing to the girl, Tom?" Ken says, taking in my disheveled appearance, my eyes puffy from crying, my bandaged hand.

How do I explain everything that just happened? How do I put words to my relief and my glee now he's here, and the pain I went through when I thought he wasn't coming, and the chaos that Tom unerringly guided me through, just as he has every time my world has threatened to fall apart since I got here?

I look at Ken and smile. "He's been putting me back together again."

9

MARY

"I missed you."

His voice is deep and rough against my ear. I am the best kind of tender and sore and swollen because it feels as though he has been inside me every minute since he returned. Our lovemaking is passionate, but it's also desperate. We need each other so badly it hurts. Even with my pussy gripping his dick, I can already feel his absence.

We're here together, but we're also so damn far away from each other. He will have to leave soon and then the distance will rush in between us. This is a little oasis in the midst of the war we've been fighting since we met. He is fighting a known enemy. My battle is a secret I keep even from him.

"I missed you too..." I gasp, my clit grinding against his pubic bone. He has me pinned on my back, his muscular body rising above me in a powerful arc. He is so fucking handsome that it hurts to look at him sometimes. I can't believe he wants me. I can't believe he's mine. This can't last forever, but for now, it's everything.

"You promise you were a good girl for Tom?"

He slides his hips back and forth in long, languid strokes as he puts me through a casual sexual inquisition.

"I was good enough," I moan. "The house is still standing, isn't it?"

"That's something," he chuckles, slipping his fingers into my mouth, giving me something to suckle on as he thrusts deep inside my wet channel. I look into his eyes and suck obediently. There's no shame with him. I am the woman he sees. I am whatever he wants me to be, and I am everything he imagines I am.

Is it a lie? If it is, this is a lie I want to live forever.

The days have passed in a wave of tangled sheets, sweat and orgasm. His hunger for me drives the darkness away, and I find shelter in his arms. I start to believe that this could be how it will be in the future. He and me together, living quiet little lives in a quiet little suburb.

"What are you thinking about?" He pulls his cock out of my pussy and drags the tip of it over my puffy lower lips.

"Nothing."

"That's not true," he says, rubbing the hot head of his cock over the bud of my clit.

"I don't know," I moan softly. "I can't even think when you do that."

He pulls away entirely, leaves my pussy aching for him. "Can you think now?"

"No," I whine, reaching for him as the cold comes in. I need his body. The hardness. The heat. The protection from the dangers we can see and those we can't. I have never been so safe before.

"You're a greedy girl," he chuckles, giving me what I want, pushing back inside me, filling me up again.

I'm not just greedy. I'm starving. I have hungered for this all my life.

KEN

It's good to be home.

Truth be told, I wasn't sure she'd be here by the time I got back. Tom's place is about as safe and suburban as you can get, and I know this girl has almost zero tolerance for either of those things.

He's done an incredible job with her though. His particular brand of discipline can be hit and miss depending on who the recipient is. I had an inkling she might take to it, but she was also so damn mad when she left Afghanistan I didn't know if she'd even give him a chance. I'm so grateful to Tom for keeping her here, keeping her alive, keeping her more or less on one piece. It's not easy to do that where this one is concerned.

I've missed her every day. But I was glad she wasn't

over there. We were exchanging fire every damn day. In the end it took reinforcements and a sustained campaign to retake the area. I've seen a lot of death lately. I desperately needed to see life. Needed to be here, in this sanctuary Tom's made. Needed to be with her.

I have a month of leave. It's not going to be enough time, but we're going to have to make it enough time. We're going to have to somehow try to fit as much of each other into the next few weeks as possible. Judging by the fact she refuses to leave my side for even a second, I think she wants the same thing.

So far, she's had three weeks with Tom. That's three times what she had with me, and they've obviously been bonding. I can't help but have a spark of jealousy, because I'm here for a month and then I'll be gone again.

That's not enough for her. It's literally not sufficient company, love, or care. She needs Tom, and I think he needs her too. But he can't give her what I can.

Right now she's curled up so tightly with me, her arm wrapped around me like she's afraid I'm going to disappear out from under her.

Beneath the sheets, my cum is leaking from between her thighs. She's covered in a light sheen of sweat, mine and hers. I couldn't resist having her almost as soon as I got back. She was just as desperate for me as I was for her. We fucked like rabbits, probably chased Tom out of his house with the noises we were making.

When she wakes up, I'll make love to her again. And again. We don't have much time together, but I'm going to make the most of it.

For now, I lie here next to her, just watching her sleep. I have never loved any woman like I love Mary. There's something that connects us. Something that distance and war and time can't break. I want to be with this woman forever.

Every time I left the military in the past, I got pulled back in. That's not going to happen again. For the first time in my life, I can't wait to be a civilian. It's going to be my turn to be a lover and a husband. We'll get our own house together. We'll get a dog. Maybe we'll adopt a kid or something down the track. We have our whole lives ahead of us, and I can't wait to live mine with her.

I've just got to get through this last stage of deployment. And she's got to survive without me. Though she has help in that department. Tom has been feeding her well, I can tell. She has a healthier glow about her, her skin and her hair look better than they did, though not being in the vicious Afghanistan climate would help with that too.

The need to pee and a growling in my stomach finally makes me get up and leave her curled up and sleeping in bed.

Tom is cooking us all dinner. He's such a fucking good guy. Always has been. Was a huge loss when he retired, but as a medic he'd seen enough carnage to last him a lifetime, and not just the enemy, but our boys, and civilians of all ages. He's retreated here to live a comfortable life, and I hope I haven't fucked that up for him too much.

"Hey man."

"Hey. Sleep good?"

"Yeah."

He hands me a beer and we sit in the silence men sit in when they're comfortable with each other.

"She's looking good."

"Good," he says.

There's a long silence. He used to cook steak when I came home, until I pointed out that the searing can smell like other things. Now he puts on a sea food spread. There's lobster already cooked and waiting, making my mouth water.

"That hospital she talks about being in…" Tom says. "Tell me it's not still…"

"Gone," I reply. "Very, very gone."

"And the doctors?"

"Also very gone."

"Good."

"Has she been okay?" I change the subject to escape the lie. I couldn't do a fucking thing about that hospital. It was running at the allowance of several governments, a dark place where they could do their dark shit. But Tom needs to hear that it's gone, or it will eat him alive. He's too good a man for that, so I keep the darkness of the details to myself. In my line of work, I've found a thousand pockets of hell here on earth. Sometimes we can take them out. Sometimes we have to let them be. It destroys good men.

"She's done her best," he says, a diplomatic answer. "She's told me some of the things that happened to her, and frankly, given those, I think she's doing incredible."

"Yeah," I agree.

"She never lays down and lets the world just roll over her," he says, that tone of admiration in his voice. "Hardest thing about dealing with her is getting her to let you look after her."

"Oh yeah," I agree again. "That's the whole reason I had to ship her out. Girl was going to try to win the war with nothing but her two fists."

We both snort with amusement.

"You going to re-enlist when this tour's over?"

"No."

He nods.

"Finally found something better, huh?"

I want to be with Mary. I want to be there for her. She's been hanging in there, and Tom has been doing his best, but it's me she really needs.

"Another six months," I say with a stretch. "And then I'll be out and back here, making your lives hell."

"Good," he smirks. "Now go be greedy with your girl while you can. Dinner will be ready soon."

I don't need to be told twice.

10

KEN

We needed toilet paper. I wanted beer. There was no reason to think that running to the store was going to be a problem, so I did it, because that's what normal civilian people do. People who aren't constantly looking over their shoulders for terrorists.

I can tell that Mary is enjoying the semblance of normality. Sometimes we exchange little smiles, shared and unspoken thoughts as to how strange and how good it is to pretend that the world is a safe place.

But we are pretending. And I'm reminded of that the second I pull back up to the house. Something is wrong. All the blinds are shut, and that's just weird because Tom loves having the sun shining in. There are also several near new vehicles I don't recognize whatsoever parked in the vicinity. This, in a neighborhood where you can be fined for leaving your vehicle in the driveway. Whoever has been parking isn't familiar with our ways and customs, and prefers rental vehicles.

I leave the beer and TP in the car and draw my gun before I go into the house, but the moment I walk through the door, I realize how useless it is. Tom is sitting on the couch, a black eye coming up on the right side of his face. Mary is cable tied to a chair and gagged.

The sight makes me want to murder every single one of the assholes who are standing in my brother's house, but I restrain the impulse for the moment. Something is happening here. Something I need to understand.

The leader of the intruders is a youngish, pale faced man with ultra blonde hair and blue eyes. When he speaks, he has a noticeable German accent.

"We haff been expecting you, Ares."

"Yeah?"

I grit my teeth and I wait for the explanation which seems to be forthcoming.

"I am Herr Schnitzenwiess," he says, speaking with clipped, efficient formality. "We are doing you the courtesy of letting you know that we are removing a spy from your midst. You have a reputation as a man well versed in the art of extractions, so it is best you know this now, before it happens. We would not like to kill a brave man such as yourself unnecessarily if you were to be foolish enough to come after us."

What the fuck is going on?

"A spy?"

He gestures toward Mary. "This woman's name is not Mary Brown. It is Ekaterina Akova. She is a Russian spy. We previously caught her attempting to infiltrate our facility in Chile, and took her prisoner. You released her, and in doing so, released something very dangerous into the world."

Mary is not a spy. She is the least spy-like person I know. Spies are subtle and calm and calculating. Like this asshole in front of me.

"I thought she was a journalist."

"She vas not a journalist," he says, occasionally slipping into the German V for W sound. "She was a spy. Raised a spy."

I smirk and shake my head. "That girl is many things. But I can tell you now, she's not a spy. She has the subtlety of a bulldozer and the stealth of a fireworks display."

"Ve did not say she was a very good spy," he says flatly.

This is ridiculous. Mary is not a spy. But if Mary isn't a spy, then why the fuck are there foreign security agents standing in my brother's house? And if I don't believe them, then why aren't I calling the cops?

I look at her. They've gagged her, but I can see something hunted and haunting in her eyes. Something that speaks volumes. Sometimes, when you hear the truth, it seems like something you should have recognized all along. Maybe even something you did know, but tried to ignore.

A tear is slipping down her cheek. That tear tells me

more than any of the words this little shit is spewing at me.

"We are taking her. Do not try to find her again. That would be a severe mistake on your part."

"You can't have her," I say, firmly. The odds aren't great. There are two of them to every one of us and she's tied up and only I'm armed but I will die before I let the same people who tortured her for months take her again, no matter what she is or isn't.

"You want to keep her? For what? You want to keep her like a kitten in your garden? She is a tigress, and she should be locked up for the greater good. We had her contained, until you were contacted by an intermediary for the KGB and sent in to play Rambo."

"You were experimenting on people there."

"Zat is not the point," he says. "You think your own government doesn't have testing facilities? You think they do not need to know precisely how new nerve agents, toxins, biological actors affect the human system? You think they do not carry out any testing at all? Or perhaps you think all that stalled back in the 60's and since then they have only been vorking out how to distill the essences of rainbows?"

I do not need his sarcasm

"I'm pretty fucking sure we don't have hospitals full of people held against their will being used as test subjects," I growl.

"You do not know, because you are not paid to know," he says. "You are paid to be Rambo and you are a very good Rambo, but you are no spymaster, and she is no little girl."

Tom lets out a low growl.

"Oh yes, ve heard how you spoke to her. Very sweet. Like baby talking a grenade," he smirks. "You had your fun, gentlemen. You had your use of her. We will finish with her."

"What do you mean?"

"She is far too dangerous to live. She will be deconstructed and disposed of."

"You mean you're going to torture and kill her. I can't allow that."

"You have no choice," he snaps, voice cold, his eyes almost reptilian in their inhuman disconnection. "We have evidence of you acting in accord with Russian agents. We have evidence of you taking one along on your duties, and then sending her home to infiltrate the homeland from your brother's house. If I were to so much as breathe a word of this to your command, you would not just be discharged. You would spend the rest of your existence in a military prison. Your brother would likely be charged with treason too. You would both serve life sentences. And in aid of what? A spy who lied to you every moment of every day you knew her?" He gives a derisive snort. "We own you. You will do as you are told."

The rage I feel is unspeakable. These men need to know they can't do this. I suspect they already do. This attempt to talk to me, get me to let them take her, it's an effort to avoid the bloodbath they know will follow if I'm not on board with it. Smart on their part, but it's not going to work.

"I won't let you kill her. If you kill her, I promise you I will destroy everything you stand for, and I will not be taken alive. I will go down fighting in her name. I'm not afraid to die, nor is Tom. So give us our girl, and get the fuck out of my brother's house."

"Men are always so villing to die for vomen," he sighs. "You are a pitiful cliche."

"I'm a pitiful cliche with enough ammunition to shred you until there's nothing left," I say, my voice like cold steel. "And I know you don't represent any current government. You don't represent anything. The only reason I'm going to let you walk out of here today is because Tom just got his carpets cleaned."

It's not a joke. Killing them would make a mess. Turn this place into a crime scene. Expose us all. These people do not represent the German government. They're a splinter group from a time gone by. They're the incarnation of an evil that will not die. I have killed many men like these. I will kill many more. But not today. Today is about keeping Mary and Tom safe, not shedding their worthless blood.

"So brutal," he laughs. "You want to be responsible for a Russian agent, Ares? Very well. You take responsibility for her. You continue your treasonous activities, which can only end in chaos and death. You will remain at my disposal if you do not wish to be reported. I will refrain from that for the moment. Give you a chance to cool down and think more clearly. She will only bring you pain."

With that, they leave, just file out of the house, leaving Mary bound on the chair. Tom and I rush for her. I cut the ties off her, pull the gag out of her mouth, and pull her into a hug.

She's crying her eyes out as I hold her.

"I'm so fucking sorry," she sobs. "I'm so sorry."

"Easy," Tom says. "Take a breath. You're safe."

"I'm not safe. None of us are. I told you that you shouldn't let me stay here."

The tears course down her cheeks. She looks utterly miserable and defeated.

"So it's true, what they said," I say, flatly, pulling back a little. Shit. Fuck. Goddamn. Part of me wishes she'd just denied it.

"It's true enough," she cries as Tom sits on the floor and pulls her into his arms, practically cradling her like a baby. This isn't the typical way to hold an interrogation, but it's an interrogation nonetheless. I need to know what the truth is, and I need it now. No more lies.

"Mary, enough," I growl. "We don't have time for hysterics. Calm down and talk to me."

"Easy," Tom says, raising a brow.

"They were right. She's not a little girl, she's…"

"I don't care what she is, she's my little girl," Tom rumbles back at me. "And we have a minute for her to calm down in."

I get up and start pacing. Time really is of the

essence. If everything that agent just told me was true, then we are capital F fucked.

Tom is doing a decent job of calming her down. A better job than I would. I only know one way to deal with spies. My training is telling me to tie her back in a chair and not stop questioning her until I'm sure she's stopped lying, but I don't want to treat Mary that way, and thankfully Tom wouldn't let me anyway. She's lucky she has both of us, because I'm at war with myself right now.

"Is it true? You're a spy?" I repeat the question when she's composed enough to talk. "Shall we call you Ekaterina now?"

"No," she says through her tears. "I'm Mary to you. I want to be Mary to me too."

Right now, I don't care what her damn name is. I want to know what's going on.

"I was raised here. My parents were Russian," she admits, her words spilling out in a fast tumbling confession. "They raised me as a sort of sleeper agent. I didn't want to be, but you don't really get a choice."

So she is a spy. And has been one her entire life. I have been fucking a goddamn Russian spy.

"And Chile?"

"They wanted me to infiltrate that hospital posing as a college kid on holiday, but I guess the Germans had a better idea of who I was than the US did. Because I got caught. So yeah, technically I'm a spy and a traitor and everything else they called me. But you're right. I'm not a very good one."

I take a sharp breath. This is just as bad as I thought. "Not being a very good spy isn't a defense against treason."

She wipes her eyes and I see her old composure return as she pulls away from Tom and stands up on her own two feet. She lifts her chin, bravely and tells me exactly what I don't want to hear.

"I know. I'm sorry. You should turn me in. Let me go to jail here. It's better than what the Germans or Russians would do to me. And you might get to keep some of your career, or at least not end up in prison too."

She deserves to go to jail. Everything I fight for, everything I uphold is completely turned upside down simply by her existence. I love her more than anything, but the right thing to do is to turn her ass in, just like she says.

"It was really nice," she says, tears filling her eyes. "It was nice being loved. It was nice feeling like I had a life, even just for a few weeks. Thank you. I won't forget it."

Is this a manipulation? Is it another lie? I want to believe her, but she's never told me a damn thing I needed to know and she's only telling me this now because her hand was forced. How many other secrets has she been keeping from me?

"You're not going to jail," Tom says.

I can't agree. She might be going to prison for a very long time. I can't really see a way out of it. It wasn't just the Chile mission. She also got an embed position in Afghanistan. How much information was she funneling to the Russians then? And did she attack that guy in the village just to get out? How much of what she's done is deliberate, and how much is just a scared girl trying to survive? I don't know, and that bothers me.

"I am," she says. "Because I have to."

"Why?"

She looks from him to me. "Because you won't ever know how sorry I really am until you see that I'm prepared to take the consequences of my actions. Report me, Ken. Take me in and turn me over. You know you have to."

"Stay here," I grind out. I need space to think and I have work to do. "And I do really mean stay fucking here. If I find you've put so much as a finger outside, you'll be in a black site before you know it."

"Jesus, Ken," Tom swears, getting to his feet. "Go easy on her."

I can't go easy on her. I don't have that luxury. "You go easy on her," I say. "And enjoy it. Be glad one of us can."

MARY

I don't blame Ken for hating me. I'm literally the very thing he has spent his life fighting. He must think everything I ever said and did with him was a lie. I can't stop crying, even though I know my tears are mostly ones of self-pity. I feel sorry for myself, sorry for what I've lost. Sorry that the past I never wanted has caught up with me and ruined absolutely everything.

What happened today is what I've been afraid of since I got back to California. I never reported back to my handlers after I got to Afghanistan. I wanted to drop off the grid. I wanted to die, in one way or another. But then Ken found me and then he sent me here and now I have something to live for.

It's not the Russians who have come for me either. And it's not actually the Germans. They look German, they sound German, but they are not affiliated in any real sense. They are a splinter from the gates of hell and they came here to reclaim me.

When they walked through that door, I felt as though my heart stopped. I recognized them instantly, not by their faces, but by their bearing. Those agents are cold, hard men with no souls whatsoever. It was like seeing the devil and his demons file in to take me away.

But Ken stood up for me in the short term, anyway, and I'll forever be grateful for that. I'd rather serve my inevitable sentence in a US prison. As bad as things might get there, they're nothing on what was done to me before and what would be done to me again.

"Don't worry," Tom says. He's trying to be reassuring. It's not working. I can feel his arms around me, but they don't feel as real as they used to. My mind is already shifting from a mode where I can be safe and secure and feel affection, to one where the only thing that matters is being numb.

"Can you stop, please?"

"Can I stop what?" Tom quirks a brow at me.

"Stop trying to make this better. I'm a fucking Russian spy. You should be reacting like Ken is. You should hate me."

"Why?"

"Because I lied to you."

He looks at me steadily. "Did you?"

"I mean, I didn't tell you who I really am. I didn't tell you why I really ended up in that hospital, or why I was in Afghanistan."

"I didn't ask you any of those things."

"So you don't mind being lied to by omission?"

"I knew you were in trouble, Mary. It's been written all over you from the moment we met. And you did try to warn me. You offered to leave a half-dozen times, always saying you were more trouble than you were worth. You told me what I needed to know, even if you think you didn't."

I can't believe him. I can't believe he doesn't hate me. I almost can't stand how good he is. It makes me want to ugly cry, but I have to try to compose myself. Just like Ken said. Now is not the time for crying.

"You should hate me," I repeat.

"Nope," he stays firm. "Not going to happen.

He wraps his arms around me, pulls me into his lap, and holds me. I don't know how long we sit there like that, time ticking away. I feel like my world is ending one breath at a time. Whatever happens next cannot be good.

———

"Come on, Mary. It's time to go."

Ken is back. He is composed and calm. I hate that, because I know what it means. It means he doesn't need me anymore. It means he's prepared to let me go to my fate.

Tom lets me up and presses a kiss to my forehead. "Be good, little girl."

"I will be," I say, wrapping my arms around his neck to give him one last hug. He feels so good, so safe. I hope I get to see him again, though I know in all likelihood I never will. I can see that in his eyes too. This is goodbye, and it's happening so quickly neither of us can properly process it.

"Where are we going? Am I going to jail?" I ask Ken the question as we get out to his car.

"I don't know."

It's hardly a reassuring response, but then again, I hardly deserve reassurance.

"Put this on."

He hands me a dark hood. A big black cloth bag. Usually this is the sort of thing that gets shoved over your face. He's at least doing me the honor of letting me put it on myself.

I pull it over my head, breathe deep through the cloth that blacks out the world.

"I'm sorry, Ken."

He grunts as he starts the car.

It's too late for sorries. I just wish he could pretend

that it wasn't. But I guess we're done with pretending now. He knows what I am. An enemy. A traitor. A spy.

It's a relief, in a way, to no longer be hiding everything from him. I've known since we met that I don't deserve him, and that the loving would end soon enough. Now that the end is here, I feel a kind of peace. If he were to put a bullet in the back of my head right now, I wouldn't blame him for it. I'd consider it a mercy.

"You can shoot me," I say. "It's okay."

He doesn't even dignify that with a response. I guess execution isn't on the menu tonight. Or at least, not in his car.

———

An hour or so later, I am taken from the car, ushered through some place I don't know. It smells like bleach, rarely an encouraging scent. Could be an abattoir. Could be a gym. Could be a hospital. I'd rather the abattoir.

"Listen to me, Mary," Ken says as he pushes me down into a hard chair. "You're about to talk to someone. Someone very important. Tell her everything. And I do mean, everything. She will know if you're lying."

I hear him walk away. Then I hear high heels enter the room. The hood is removed from my head and I find myself looking into the steely gaze of a very stern looking lady in her fifties. Her silver streaked hair is pulled back from her face and she has a demeanor about her that I find even more frightening than Ken.

She doesn't introduce herself. She sits down in front of me and starts asking questions in the sort of way people do when they have your life in their hands.

This is the end of the line. I am all out of chances. I am all out of hope. There's no point in lying anymore. I have nothing left to protect.

So I talk to her. I tell her everything. I confess my sins and crimes and she listens to them all, neither overtly judging or giving any kind of sign which would let me know how this is being received. I'm sure Ken is listening too, learning every terrible thing about me.

It's a real possibility that I'll be spending the rest of my life behind walls like these. I may never see the light of day again. But I'll always have the memory of Tom as he holds me over his knee and spanks me as if I'm still a girl who can be saved.

KEN

Everything that ever took place between Mary and I was a lie.

It hurts, but it's the truth and I have to accept it. The number of things I knew about her could have been counted on one hand, and now I'm pretty certain at least half of them were untrue.

These are the things I know about her for sure:

She is a spy.

She is a professional liar.

She is a traitor to everything I believe in.

These are the facts of the matter. I have been sleeping with the enemy.

I am angry. I am disappointed. In her and in myself. I should have known something was wrong. I did know something wasn't right with her, but I always put it down to her broken past. I just didn't know how broken it really was. I thought I could love her better, but there are some things love can't fix.

That doesn't mean I'm giving up on her. Not at all. It means that our relationship is about to change in a serious way.

There's separation between government and military. But there's also a gray area in between, and in that gray area there are a series of branches hardly anybody nobody knows about. Task-forces, spies, special forces units, all acting under the cover of total anonymity and ultimate deniability. I have been engaged with several of them, from time to time. I guess Herr Fuckwad didn't know that.

Mary was right about needing to be turned in. She's in the kind of trouble you cannot get out of on your own. Her whole life has been a lie, in many respects. Her childhood a facade, her adolescence a farce. I feel for her, but she fucked herself and she fucked me when she didn't tell me the truth when she had the chance.

Now we're on the back foot and entirely at the mercy of the woman behind the glass. A real spymaster. They call her the Head. She runs a small group which might be able to provide Mary with salvation - but it's not going to be easy, even if the Head agrees to take her on.

They've been talking for a while, though I'm sure the Head managed to get everything she needed to out of Mary in the first two minutes of their conversation.

I'm being allowed to watch this for a very good reason, so I pay attention. Make sure I hear everything Mary says. The events she details are not pleasant. She has been through even more than I knew. That, of course, is because she chose not to tell me. She's a little vault of secrets, that girl, all of them bad.

For weeks and weeks on end, she kept secrets so dangerous it could have gotten us all killed. At first I felt betrayed, but as I listen to her talk, I understand why she did it.

She doesn't know how to trust. Doesn't know how to give up control, or how to surrender. There were so many ways I could have, should have taught her that lesson. But I didn't. And now, she's going to pay the price.

MARY

I talk for what feels like forever. I tell the lady about what happened in Chile. And then I tell her what happened before Chile. How people would come to see me at college and give me little tasks to do that seemed so innocuous. I tell her about what happened after Ken

174

saved me, how I fucked everything up and then suddenly I had papers for Afghanistan. Didn't matter that I knew I wasn't really a journalist. By that time I was just glad to have something to do. Didn't matter if I died. A lot of what I've told Ken over the weeks is true. But I've omitted other things. Things that happened to me, things I did. I sold drugs. I took drugs. I have been captured twice by dealers since he rescued me and managed to escape both times.

The woman listens. Sometimes she asks questions. I answer as best I can. But then, in the end, I run out of words. And as the silence falls, I know my judgement is imminent. Any moment now, I will feel the cold steel of cuffs on my hands, and I will be taken to the kind of cell you never leave.

She steeples her hands. "Mary," she says. "You have shown a remarkable lack of judgement over the years, only made up for by sheer tenacity and what one might call dumb luck. Your association with your Russian handlers has made you a traitor by all reasonable definitions, and yet your loyalty to them can hardly be verified as you seem to have made no contact whatsoever after obtaining passage to Afghanistan. In short, you are a spy who has never actually spied to any successful extent."

That sounds about right. I've been used in a hundred ways, but I've managed to avoid being useful in any of them. Unfortunately, that doesn't help me much now. I'm still a criminal, a liar and a traitor.

"I've spoken extensively with Ares," she continues.

"He has provided his impressions and assessment of you, which of course, has to be tempered with the personal component of your relationship. He may not be the most objective source, but I note he did expel you from Afghanistan when he thought necessary, and he did bring you to us immediately upon discovering your identity, so I do still trust his judgement where you are concerned."

It's probably easy for him to judge me. He must hate me so much now. He's not like Tom. He's not sentimental. I'm pretty sure once you cross Ken, that's the end of it. He's done with me, I'm sure.

"I've made my decision, Miss Brown."

Oh shit. Here it comes. The cuffs and the cell.

"From this moment onwards, you are property of the United States of America. You are an asset. You do not have the rights or protections of a citizen. You can and likely will be called on to do dangerous work, which we will expect you to be competent in."

Shit. I've heard this talk before. This is the talk they give you when they tell you they can kill you at any moment. At this point, I almost wish they would. I have screwed my life up a thousand time over. Some things can't be un-fucked. This is one of them.

"I'm really not a very good spy though…"

"You will be. Ares has been reassigned. He will be your handler. He will make sure you carry out missions assigned to you with competency. You will answer to him in every way. Do you understand?"

I can't believe what I'm hearing. My punishment is going to be… belonging to Ken?

"He wants me?"

"Consider yourself very, very lucky, young lady," she says. "He requested this course of action. I was disinclined to grant it, but all things considered, I am willing to give you a chance. You must realize that there will not be others."

Gratitude overwhelms me. I can't believe that I am really being give another chance. Ken must have called in a lifetime of favors to swing this one. "Oh my god, thank you! Thank you so much!"

She smiles tightly, and it doesn't reach her eyes. "Don't thank me just yet, Miss Brown. You now fall under a very strict hierarchy, and I can promise you here and now that you will not find the leniency, nor the leeway you experienced under your previous handlers."

"Well they didn't really…"

"Precisely," she says, her lips thinning. She lifts her voice a little. "Ares, you may come collect your material."

Material. I'm just stuff to this woman. Like a bag of old socks, but I don't care because I'm free - well, sort of, and I'm Ken's.

I smile as he comes into the room. He doesn't smile back. He looks at me with an expression which sends a chill right through to the very core of me. Has he stopped loving me? No. I don't believe that. He wouldn't have asked to keep me if he hated me. This is his professional facade. The mask he needs to wear. It's a frightening one to be sure.

"Come with me," he says, beckoning me. I get up and do as I'm told. From here on out, this is my life. I literally owe him my obedience. There's no question in my mind about doing what he says. He saved me. He saved me from those who were trying to hurt me, and in the end, he's saved me from the destiny that was picked out for me before I was even conceived. There will be no more lies between us. I swear that to myself. I'll never lie to him again.

———

Ken and I leave the room together. I never thought I'd see him again, and now I'm right by his side. I couldn't have asked for a better outcome.

"Thank you so much, Ken."

"Sir."

"What?"

"Call me sir."

Oh shit. So that is how this is going to be.

"We're not going back to Tom's house, I guess."

"No," he says, turning to look down at me. "This is a secure facility where you will start your training with me. This is going to be your home for the next year at least."

He seems so different now. Colder. Sterner. Harsher.

"But what about Tom?"

"I'll tell Tom where you are."

"Can I see him?"

"When you've earned it."

"What about him? What about what he wants?"

"No more questions," he snaps in final tones. That voice he's using is one he's only used on me a handful of times. It's the voice of command. The one that tells me what I want doesn't matter and I need to do as I'm damn well told.

I have Ken, but I don't have the Ken I used to have. I used to have a lover. Now I have a handler.

11

MARY

It turns out that my premonitions were not entirely inaccurate. I spend the night in a cell. Alone.

My impressions of the site is that I'm somewhere which is a cross between a gym and a jail. There are tall gates and bright lights and the atmosphere is wildly oppressive. If I hadn't spent several months being taken apart in an experimental hospital, I might be intimidated. As it is, I know how much worse this could be and I'm grateful.

The people here have obviously been alerted to my arrival. They have a remarkably spacious six by six cell waiting for me, complete with toilet, shower and heavy steel door. It's not exactly homey, but once again, could be so much worse.

Ken puts me in there with hardly a word. If Tom were here, he'd probably still read me a bedtime story and tuck me in. I get the idea that it's going to be a long time before that happens again. A plastic mattress and pillow are all the comfort I'm getting.

"Night," I say softly, trying not to be weak. He'll hate me for weakness now, almost as much as I'll hate myself.

"See you in the morning," he says.

"0300?"

He doesn't reply, just walks away. He saved my life again, but apparently that doesn't stop him from being angry. Or maybe this is just how handlers treat their 'material'. I really don't know.

———

I don't sleep very well that night. Part of it is because I'm reflecting on the utter clusterfuck of my life. Part of it is missing home. Missing Tom. Missing Ken. I hope Ken is in a better mood tomorrow.

I close my eyes, and what feels like a second later, I'm awake again. Ken is standing over me. I get the sense that it's early. Whatever time it is, I'm just so relieved to see him that at first I almost forget why he's here and what we're doing.

"Get up, Brown."

He's not in a better mood.

"Hello, sir," I say, hoping the *sir* earns me a few points. I get out of bed too. It's not like I'm missing much lying there.

"Take your clothes off."

Usually when Ken wants my clothes off, he takes them off for himself.

"Why?"

He gives me a hard look. He is wearing a black sweater, pants, and combat boots. He looks ready for anything. He also looks fucking hot, as usual. I have to start seeing past how handsome he is though or this is going to be pure torture.

Under his hard bicolor gaze, I get naked and drop my clothes in the bag he provides me.

"If you'd done as you were told, I would have given you these," he says, hefting a pair of overalls which he took out of the bag I put my clothes in. But, because you answered back, you get nothing."

"Nothing?"

He walks to the door and opens it before gesturing to me with his head.

"Step out, Brown."

He expects me to walk around this facility naked? I must not be understanding him. He can't possibly want me to be naked. Especially as he knows exactly how I feel about my body. Being seen unclothed is bad enough when you have a normal-ish body. It's unthinkable when you look like the bride of Frankenstein.

"Give me something to wear."

"You forfeited the right to clothing. Now hurry up, before the others come on duty. Unless you want to be seen."

"Oh fuck you." My temper flares. This is ridiculous.

This isn't how you train people... or maybe it is. Special forces go through some real fucking hazing in their training. I bet Ken's been through a lot worse than this. Doesn't mean I intend to put up with it.

"No," he growls. "There's not going to be any fucking, Brown. You've seen to that by hiding things from me and making this a matter of national security."

I suppose I can't be surprised he's throwing that in my face.

"So I guess I was pretending not to be a spy, and you were pretending not to be an asshole," I bite at him.

"Out. Now." He jerks his head toward the door again. I cross my arms over my chest, hiding a small percentage of the scars that marr me.

"Or what?"

"What part of being my material didn't you understand girl?"

"I might be your material, but I haven't been given a lobotomy. Give me the goddamn overalls."

Now, of course, he can't give me them. If he backs down now I win and he loses, and that's no way to start whatever this is off on the right foot.

Ken strides toward me, scoops me up over his shoulder, and carries me out of the cell, butt ass naked. He called my bluff alright. Jesus. What the fuck. As he strides down the hall, I start attempting to negotiate.

"Ken, come on, I'm sorry, okay? I'll do what you say next time. I get it. I fucked up."

"You're right about that, girl. And it's sir."

He sets me down in a gym. Points at a treadmill. "Start running."

He's trying to humiliate me, and I don't understand why. So I wasn't immediately obedient. So what?

"Start. Running."

I stare at him. "What are you going to do if I don't?"

Ken leans down, his eyes locked on mine. "You have been given one chance, Mary. One chance to be something more than what you are. To make what you did wrong right. Most people never get this chance. So how about you get on the damn treadmill and start running instead of giving me attitude."

"I don't care."

"What?" He jerks his head back, surprised.

He doesn't get it. I didn't agree to this because I wanted a second chance at life. I agreed to it because I wanted a second chance with him. If this means I can't have him, or if it means I end up hating him, then I don't want it. It's just not worth staying around for.

"If this is how you're going to be, I don't want a second chance. Get someone to put a bullet in me. This isn't fucking worth it."

Ken swears under his breath. "Goddamn you are a pain in the ass, little girl."

In those two last words, I hear the love he still has for me, and I can already see the frustration on his face. He's doing what he thinks he needs to. Apparently, being an asshole is integral to making me a good spy. Hell. Maybe it is. What do I know.

"Fine," I say. "I'll get on the treadmill."

He straightens up and watches me as I get on, still entirely naked. And I start running.

KEN

This is going to be even more difficult than I imagined it would be. It's a nice morning and I would much rather be at home in bed with her than barking orders at her, but that is where we are now. The moment the Germans walked in, my life as I knew it evaporated. I can't be her lover anymore. I can barely be her friend. Tom thinks it's hard not being able to see her. He doesn't understand how fucking brutal it is to be right next to her and be unable to hold her or comfort her because the process won't work if she's coddled through it.

She looks good on the treadmill. A few months ago, being naked in front of me was something she could barely handle. Now she's exposing herself with a degree of pride, wearing those scars like a badge of honor. They remind me that she's a survivor, and even though she lacks discipline, she's got all the strength she needs for this, and more besides.

"It's too late to say sorry, isn't it," she says as she runs.

"Much too late."

There's a flash of hurt and sadness in her eyes. I want to pull her down and comfort her and tell her everything will be okay, but Tom and I have done nothing but comfort her and tell her everything will be okay, and the result was she lied to us.

Mary doesn't understand kindness. It isn't processed in her brain the way it should be. When people are nice to her, she thinks they're weak, or stupid, or both. Her experiences have damaged her more deeply than the scars that run her body. They've rewired her ability to relate.

She lied to me every moment she was with me and it was no effort at all, because lying comes naturally to her. It's how she's survived her entire life.

Most people need to be trained how to behave. She needs to be trained to feel. The Head and I have discussed this a lot, formulated an approach which I hope like hell works, because I am going to have to be the villain in this.

The alternative was to hand her over to someone else. Someone who wouldn't understand her. Someone who would try all the tricks to break her and fail and probably get him or herself killed in the process.

Mary is dangerous. Not in the way most people in our field are. It's not that she's particularly lethal in an offensive situation. But she's proven time and time again that she is the kind of survivor you do not want to underestimate.

I made that mistake. I thought I knew her because we were intimate. I didn't know her at all. She was keeping everything back from me because she was afraid of the consequences of honesty.

That is no longer an option for her. I will strip away

her ability to hide and I will force her to see that I don't abandon her even though I know who and what she is.

Even now, on the treadmill, her breasts bouncing with every stride, she's got an expression of self control. She thinks I want obedience. She's wrong.

I want everything.

MARY

"Faster!"

In a world where Ken rules, the consequence of being slow is pain. Right now he has a long cane in his hand, one he whips across my ass when I miss the timer. There are six points on the floor, each of them three feet apart. Every few seconds, one of them will light up. I need to be on it within a fraction of a second, or he whips the cane against my bare ass. Because I'm naked. Of course.

This probably isn't in any official training manual, but I can already feel what it's doing. Doesn't take a genius to work out that I'm being programmed to follow his cues, react to his voice, do precisely what he says, when he says it, regardless of how outwardly pointless it is.

"Again!"

"Ow!"

It's been weeks of this, and Ken has proved himself a harsh taskmaster. No sex. No intimacy. Just bending to his will in a hundred different ways. Learning at his knee, but not over it. God I wish he'd just spank me, but he knows I want that. This cane is the closest thing he's given me to it, and I hate it because it's so distant from him.

I want his hands on my body. I want to feel like I've earned his forgiveness and his trust. I don't know if I'll ever earn either of them. I was a liar for too long.

"Too slow."

"OW!" The cane lands again, biting the soft skin of my ass with a painful welting stroke.

"Keep going!" He barks the order at me harshly.

I shoot him an angry look. He stares back, so fucking handsome, so commanding, so utterly in control. And then the lights change again, and the cane cuts down across my ass again, another thick welt of pain lighting my nervous system on fire.

This is inhumane, but I'm not human to anyone here. I'm an animal to be trained. All stick, no carrot.

I think it's over between us. I think I might have lost him forever. The only thing left to lose is myself.

I stop moving. I stand stock still. The lights flash. The cane comes down. I ignore it. I can block out pain. I still feel it, but it doesn't touch me the way it should.

Ken gives me two more whacks and then comes to stand over me, looming tall and imposing above me.

"What are you doing, Brown?"

"Giving up. It's what you want me to do. Right."

"Sort of," he says. "Not like this though."

"What does that even mean?"

"It means do as you're told," he growls. "You've missed the sequence."

"I don't give a shit about the sequence."

His eyes flash. I can feel the intensity of his displeasure. I know he's angry. Before he found out about my secret, he'd do something about this. He'd throw me over his knee. He'd bend me over and fuck me. He'd do something to show me who is boss.

But he won't do that now. Because he doesn't care about me anymore. Because I'm a job.

"You want to spend the next twenty-four hours locked down in your cell, Brown?"

"Make it forty-two," I snap back. "Hell, make it forever."

A cold smirk passes over his lips. "Goddamn, Brown, you're one tough little girl, aren't you."

I'm exactly as tough as I need to be. I don't want to be tough. I want to be soft. I want to be small again and curl up with him and Tom and be held between them. But I'm losing hope of that ever happening again.

"Start the sequence again," he says, pointing toward the flashing lights.

"Or what?"

"There is no or what, Brown. There's just doing what I say. Start the sequence again."

He's utterly immovable. I barely recognize him right now. Is this really the man who used to kiss me so thoroughly I felt it all the way to my toes? Or am I just seeing the real Ken now, not the charade of the man he presented to me?

I don't know what's real or what's not. I don't know what to do. I don't know how to fix my many mistakes.

He points to the lights. I move back toward them. Not because I want to. Not because I think it will please him. Just because there's nothing else to do.

———

Half an exhausting hour later, he's finally satisfied.

"Okay, you're done. Go grab a shower, Brown."

I wipe the sweat off my brow and try a smile. "You want to join me?"

Something flashes in his eyes. Is it desire? Is it irritation? Both?

"Don't test me," he growls. His face is like granite. His bearing is so fucking staunch it genuinely looks like he has a stick up his ass. Pointing that out would not go well for me.

"How am I testing you? I'm just asking if you want to get naked with me and stand under hot water?"

I know I'm pushing my luck. I don't really care. Having him so close to me and yet refusing to be intimate with me is killing me. I want a sign he still wants me. I want to know he's still mine.

He's impossible to read now. I don't know if he's doing this because it's his professional facade, or because he doesn't like me anymore, but whatever the reason is, it hurts like hell.

"Do you love me anymore, Ken?"

"You have two minutes to have a shower," he says blankly. "Every second you stand here is a second less you have to get clean. I'd get going if I were you."

KEN

She wants to know how I feel. That's natural and human. But she's known how I've felt since Afghanistan and all it did was allow her to hide, and if fucking her could fix the problems she has, she would have been cured a hundred times over by now.

To an outsider, this might seem cruel. To her, I seem like an asshole. I'm sure she is afraid that I don't care for her anymore, but the truth is I love her more than ever and I would love nothing more than to get into a shower with her, and spend the night with her tight little body wrapped around my cock.

Her eyes are searching my face. I see the hurt there, but there's something else too. She's a smart girl. She's looking for an angle she can use to break this process down, escape the discipline.

I wait. Seconds tick by.

"Well, Brown, looks like you're not getting a shower today."

She shrugs.

Goddamn it. She is so fucking good at resisting attempts at conditioning. It's no doubt how she survived the hospital, but now it's damn near impossible to break through to her.

My hand tightens on the cane and I swish it back and forth a few times.

She just smirks at me. She's not afraid of this. She's not scared of pain. Or of me.

"Tell me you love me and I'll do what you say," she says.

"Love isn't a bargaining chip, Brown. It's not something to hide behind. And it's not going to get you out of trouble here either."

"I'm in trouble?"

"Talking back, refusing orders. Yes, you're in trouble."

"Oh no, what are you going to do to me?"

The little brat smiles broadly, thrilled with herself. She's pushing me ever further down the path of being an unrelenting hard ass to her and she doesn't even know it.

"Drop and give me twenty, Brown!" I bark the order, raising my voice and injecting enough bass to make her flinch. "NOW!"

She slips down to her hands and knees and starts doing as she's told. Her form is sloppy from the get go, which suits me perfectly.

"Get that ass flat in line with your body," I growl, whipping the cane across the rise of her cheeks.

She lets out a squeal and a little breathy gasp. Jesus. She's enjoying this. And goddamn it, so am I. I bring the cane down again, just below the other mark. It has to burn like hell, but she takes it with another one of those grunting little groans of pleasure.

"Cut it out, Brown!"

"What?" She drops to the ground and rolls over to look up at me with a smirk on her face. "I've been a bad girl, Ken. You should punish me."

MARY

I can see his cock tenting his pants. I'm winning. He knows it too and he hates it.

With a growl, Ken drops the cane and grabs me by the hair. He yanks me up to my knees, pulling me hard against his legs. My cheek grazes the throbbing ridge of his cock and I let my mouth open, my tongue extending to lick the fabric covered ridge.

"Stop it," he growls, giving my hair a tug.

Being handled like this is making me wet. My nipple is hard, my pussy is fucking soaked. I want him so badly I can hardly stand it.

"Let me suck your cock," I whisper up at him.

"Mary…" he groans my name.

"Fuck my mouth," I add. "My pussy… or fuck my ass, just please take me."

I feel him pull me against his crotch a little harder, rubbing his dick against my cheek. And then I see a light come into his eye. One I haven't seen before. It's dark and there's a hint of cruelty.

"You want me to fuck you?"

"Yes…" I mewl the word, rubbing up against him like a kitten.

He's going to break. He's going to give into the lust between us. He's going to fuck me and then I won't be in trouble anymore.

Ken taps my cheek lightly with his fingers, a little gesture of censure.

"You haven't earned my cock," he says, shaking his

head as if I am some petulant little thing who doesn't deserve his dick.

I feel a blush creeping over me as my attempted seduction turns into a shameful desperate display. I was wrong. He's not losing control at all.

"If you want this cock, you're going to have to be a whole lot more obedient, little girl," he growls, pulling me back across his pants, my mouth almost making contact with that hard rod I so crave. "Right now, you've earned nothing at all."

I thought, for a minute, that I might be able to get back into his good graces and turn this experience into something more pleasurable for myself, but Ken is not stupid and nor is he weak willed. I can see his arousal. It's close enough to nearly taste. But it's not going to do me a damn bit of good.

He releases my hair and lets me sink back down onto the floor.

"Go have a shower, Brown," he says, giving my thigh a light tap with the end of the cane.

This time, I'm more than happy to scramble away to the seclusion of the shower. All I've done is wind myself up, and gotten absolutely nothing in the process.

12

MARY

I've made a decision. I obviously can't please Ken. I can't be what he wants me to be. The trust he had in me was shattered when the Germans walked in, and it won't ever come back. I think we both know that. He just doesn't want to admit it, because he's a fighter and he's honorable. So I'm going to relieve him of the burden. I'm going to get out of here. Tonight.

The security in this place is pretty good, but it's not really intended to hold people. It's intended to train them. And once Ken goes home every night, the staff switch out. The ones who replace him are much more relaxed. Nicer, really. They feel a bit sorry for me for being locked down all the time and sometimes they give me treats, like access to the rec room. I've never been so thrilled to be able to watch shitty tv than I have been here.

I'm going to be taking advantage of their kindness, which is shitty, but it's for the greater good. Everybody will be better off without me.

My previous handlers, the ones I didn't really even know were handlers, the men and women who were always around me in my teenage years, did teach me a trick or two. Like how to fool the kinds of scanners they use here. Fingerprints are unique to people, true, but people also leave them fucking everywhere they go. If you know what you're doing, you can make an impression of almost anybody's prints. I've taken the liberty of doing that for a few people, even Ken. Anyone who touches anything inside my room is a candidate for the technique.

I leave my room around midnight. It wasn't locked because I slipped a piece of plastic into the mechanism which allows the bolt to slide a little ways, but not all the way. If someone isn't paying attention, it looks like the cell is locked.

There aren't any patrols on, because nobody is supposed to be out until morning. I walk out what is basically the front door and into the parking lot. There's a car there. It's always there, some silver thing. It opens with a thin strip of metal pushed down the inside of the window, and the engine starts when I pull and strip the wires under the steering wheel. This is almost too easy.

The last obstacle is the main gate. But that's actually the simplest obstacle of all, because this car never gets stopped. I don't know who it belongs to, but this car has special privileges here. Whoever is monitoring the gate doesn't even look at me. The gates just open.

I'm free.

A grin spreads over my face. It really was too fucking easy, but then again, that has been my experience of life a lot of the time. Sometimes, the biggest obstacle to a thing is just daring to do it. I dared do this. And now I'm out. On the road.

I press my foot down on the accelerator and feel the thrill of freedom. Pure joy courses through my veins. I know I'm not necessarily going to get away with this, but right now it doesn't matter. The walls are gone. The world is wide open.

The smart move would be to head inland. Find a rural state. Hang out there long enough to get hold of a passport and then jet off to a foreign country where the quality of life is good. Australia, maybe. New Zealand. Somewhere nice and far.

I could head to Hawaii, or Indonesia. I could go on perpetual Safari in deep Africa.

I could go anywhere. But there's really only one place I want to go: home.

———

It's past two in the morning when I slip open my daddy's window. Tom never locks it. He likes it to be open just a little to let the fresh air in.

He stirs as I slip through the gap, but before he can

panic and yell, I flick the bedside light on and whisper to him.

"Don't worry. It's just me!"

The sleep falls from his handsome face instantly. It's been weeks since I saw him and I almost forgot how fucking handsome he is. His hair is messy from sleep. He has a five o'clock shadow which is graying just a little. He looks perfect. Shocked, but perfect.

Tom's eyes widen as he gets up and drags me into a big bear hug. I breathe his scent deep and snuggle into his arms as he holds me so damn tight. I have needed a hug for a long time. I missed him so much. I wish he could come with me, but I know he can't. I've got maybe a few minutes with him, and I just want to be held.

"What are you doing here, little girl?"

"Shhh," I put my finger to his lips. "I just wanted to say goodbye."

"Goodbye?"

"I'm leaving."

"Leaving where?"

"The state, the country, I don't know," I shrug. "I'm just leaving. But I wanted to say bye first."

Tom's arms tighten around me.

"You know Ken is in the next room, right?"

"Yeah. And I know that in about two minutes, he's going to get a call saying I've escaped. He's going to leave here and rush to the facility. When he does, I want to take your car. There's another one parked around the corner. I don't want to steal it. I want you to give it back to them when I'm gone."

Tom shakes his head.

"Little girl, I am not helping you run away."

I expected this. I need to appeal to his softer side. "Do you know what they're doing to me there? They keep me in a cell. And then Ken comes and makes me do the most ridiculous physical activities that aren't even for any reason. He just wants to hurt me."

"That is not true," Tom says. "That is absolutely not true."

"He wouldn't let me see you. He kept me locked up in a cell and he humiliated me. He made me run naked."

"And?"

I look up at Tom, shocked. "And that's horrible!"

"It sounds pretty standard for special forces. Actually, it sounds mild," Tom says. "When Ken went through, they made him dip his balls in a freezing lake for as long as he could take it. And then they did a whole lot of other stuff that made that seem like a joke."

My jaw drops. "You want them to freeze my balls?"

"You don't have balls, little girl," he says gently. "But I know what you're going through. And I know it's tough. But he's doing what he needs to. And you…" Tom lets out a small chuckle as the enormity of the situation hits him. "Oh my god did you just get yourself into trouble."

"I'm leaving," I repeat. "I'm going away."

"You absolutely are not," Tom says firmly. "You're

going to stay right here and we're going to wake Ken up and tell him. He might still be able to fix this."

"No!" I hiss in a whisper. "He's not the same man he was before. He's mean. He doesn't love me. He doesn't even like me."

Tom runs his hand over my hair, stroking it back from my forehead gently. "He's trying to get you where you need to be, baby. He can't be your lover right now."

"So I don't get love until I do what they want?" My lower lip trembles as Tom snugs me tight against his body. I need this so badly. I need him. I have craved this, and I have been denied it. Right now, I don't even care that half the reason he's holding me so tight is so I don't escape again. I close my eyes and I try to hold on to this moment. I will time to stop so that I can just stay here forever, held by a man who has never shown me anything other than complete and total care.

"You're loved, Mary," Tom murmurs. "By both of us. But you have to be a good girl."

"I have to be a good little prisoner, you mean," I snort. "I won't be. I can't be."

"What the *hell*!?"

The exclamation bursts out from behind us. I turn to see Ken standing in the doorway.

The look on his face is priceless. He's so shocked. This moment is utterly absurd in so many ways. I escaped clean and fucked it up by coming here. And now Ken's woken up from a deep sleep to find me in his brother's room. This is ridiculous. We are three utterly fucked people. All we want is to be together, but we can't because of a past none of us had any control over, but now they have to punish me for it. And themselves. How fucking stupid.

I can't help but laugh.

That might be the single biggest mistake of my life.

Ken crosses the room, grabs me by the wrist, and yanks me out of Tom's arms.

"What the hell are you doing here?" He thunders the question down at me. He's wearing nothing but boxer shorts. It's been a while since I saw his body like this, the muscular planes, the breadth of his shoulders. He's so fucking hot. Especially when he's angry. And right now, he's furious.

"I came to see Tom."

"She's running away," Tom says, dropping me right in it.

"Mary!" Ken says my name like a curse. "Mary what the hell? How did you…"

I am not telling him how I did what I did. That's for me to know and him to review on the security footage.

"Do you have any idea what would have happened if you'd actually gotten away? You could have been declared an enemy of the state!" He snarls the words at me, his fists curled in my shirt.

"Who cares?" I damn near yell back at him.

"I care, Mary. I fucking goddamn well fucking care," he swears. "Goddamn, girl."

I've never seen him this close to losing control. Ever. Anger is coming off him in waves to the point I am actually frightened. He has never harmed me before, but he might really hurt me this time.

The ground starts to slide away beneath my feet as Ken drags me out of the house and puts me into his car, picking me up and more or less tossing me inside it. "Don't fucking move," he snarls in at me, his eyes narrowed, his nostrils flared.

The car door slams shut, and I am left alone.

KEN

"Watch her," I instruct Tom before I go back inside and get dressed. It takes me no more than sixty seconds to yank my clothes on. They're sixty long, furious seconds. I can't believe Mary. She seems to make things worse for herself almost on purpose. I thought she understood that she was being given a second chance. A last chance. Apparently she understands nothing.

Tom is standing guard outside, still in his pajamas. He pulls me aside before I get into the car.

"I know you're pissed," he says. "And you have every right to be, but..."

"I don't want to hear buts right now," I growl.

"I know" he says. "And that's exactly why you need to hear one. She's a brat."

"This goes way past bratty."

"Agreed, but, Ken. She came *here*. Where she had to know she'd be caught. She ran away *to home*. She missed us."

"So? Everybody misses their families. You think we

can have a military or secret service where people just sneak off home mid-war because they need some snuggles?"

"She's been through a lot."

"I know. I know exactly what she's been through. And I know exactly what she's doing. She's proved a point. We can't hold her. She can get out whenever she wants. I've spent weeks working on this girl and it's done precisely fuck all."

I am beyond frustrated. I am angry. Deeply angry, because either I'm going to have to lie to cover for her, or she's going to likely lose her chance to be rehabilitated at all.

Tom nods and steps back. "Okay," he says. "Just know. This isn't your fault. You did your best."

His words are well intentioned but they just piss me off. This cannot be my best. Having the woman I love sitting in the car crying, waiting for me to take her back to a facility she hates to put her through training which makes me a brutal, cold taskmaster is not the best. I'd say it was the worst, but I know things can always be worse.

"I'm going to take her back, Tom. Don't wait up."

I get into the car. She's sitting next to me quietly and she doesn't say a word as I start it and get on the road. For about twenty minutes, we drive in silence, heading out of the city. As we get out of the suburbs, she tries one more time.

"We could just go."

"What?" I snap the question, my eyes never leaving the road.

"You could just drive somewhere inland. We could go and hide in the mountains. We could be together. You could not have to hate me."

Her voice is so small and so plaintive I almost feel sorry for her. But I can't. She wants to run away to escape the consequences of her actions. It's what she always does. She has no idea how to resolve trouble she finds herself in. She doesn't even seem to understand that it can be done.

"I don't hate you."

That's all I say. For the rest of the journey, we say silent. She can tell I'm taking her back, and I'm not in the mood to discuss the matter. My mind is on the near future, when we're both going to face the fallout from this little stunt.

———

Sure enough, on return I find the place lit up like the Fourth of July. There are armed guards everywhere. The moment we come to a halt inside the gates, they swarm the car and they take Mary into custody. It's like a zombie movie, except instead of brains, they just want her. She goes quietly, thank god, not that she has much choice considering how many people are on her. Took fewer people to catch Bin Laden.

I'm torn between wanting to kick the ass of everyone who dares lay a hand on her, and feeling a sense of satisfaction that she's getting the treatment she deserves.

That satisfaction doesn't last long. I'm next out of the car. And of course, someone wants to see me.

———

"How do you explain this, Ares?"

The Head is not pleased. When this woman isn't pleased, you damn well know it. She's not a tall woman, but she has a presence which can fill the room. And she's not a particularly attractive woman by merit physical features alone, but she has a steel about her which makes her unique and in her time she has bought many, many men to their knees.

I've been called into her office and I'm standing on a small rug in front of her desk like a damn schoolboy. Her hair is down, because like almost everybody else currently on site, she was called in from sleep to deal with the breach. In other words, Mary.

"Well, ma'am. It would appear that the subject took it upon herself to escape after I had left the premises."

"She stole a car."

I clear my throat. "She left it at my home. It is unharmed."

"Nevertheless, she stole a car."

"Yes," I agree. "She did."

She purses her lips and looks at me. "I'm sorry."

"Ma'am?" My heart sinks. What is she sorry about? Sorry she's going to recommend Mary be cancelled out of the program? Maybe trade her to Russia? Or some of the other interested parties?

"You made us aware that she was a high risk inmate, and unfortunately she appears to have been handled in a lax manner in your absence. I know the work you've put into her, Ares. This is a setback you didn't need. I think you should move to on-site quarters until her breaking period is complete."

I can't believe it. The Head is apologizing to me. I thought I was going to have to basically beg for Mary's life.

"You still want her in your program?" I try not to let my shock show, but fail.

"I'm aware of the condition Miss Brown is in," she says. "I'm also aware of how she came to be in that condition. She has rare qualities, Ares. They make her difficult to handle. I'm sure for many, utterly impossible. But you have formed a rapport and you have demonstrated control over her in a number of ways. We don't deal with easy people here. We keep the challenges. The drop outs from other units. We keep the people who are too much trouble for others. Because they can do things other don't - like break out in the middle of the night and take my car."

"Your car." Oh fuck. Her car. Of course it had to be her car.

"Yes, Ares. My car. I trust it will be returned in the same condition it left."

"Yes ma'am, of course."

"You're dismissed, Ares. I suggest you go make it

abundantly clear how unacceptable this evening's activities were." Her eyes twinkle. "By any means necessary."

Holy hell.

I have a newfound respect for the Head. I don't know her well, and that's by design. Nobody does. But she's the kind of woman who can provide a space for me to actually deal with Mary, and not throw her out because she's trouble. I appreciate that more than I can say.

"Oh, and Ares?"

"Yes, ma'am?"

"When you're finished with her, send her to me."

MARY

I'm locked up again. Oh well. I guess I didn't really lose anything in the escape. Except for whatever remaining shreds of trust Ken might have had in me. It's a weird feeling to be locked up again. It was nice to see Tom even though he fucked me over. That's the thing about the Ares Brothers. They play it straight. They don't bend the rules. Not ever. Definitely not for me.

I got my hug though. Worth it.

Suddenly, the door opens. Ken is standing there. He has a cane in his hand. Of course. It's the only thing he uses on me these days.

I stand up and face him, and before he can say

anything, I drop my pants and turn around. He wants my ass. He can have it.

I hear him grunt and the door closes.

He walks around me, looks me in the face. It's been a while since I really looked at Ken, saw how handsome he still is. How much passion and intelligence is held in his gaze. When he looks into my eyes, I feel a connection which remains unbroken, no matter what.

The cane rises between my legs. He presses the cool length of it between my lips along my slit. I stand stock still as one of the little ridges of bamboo nudges against my clit.

"You fucked up, girl," he says, his voice dangerously cold.

I'm more turned on than I have been in a very long time. If this is what happens to me when I fuck up, I'm going to fuck up every damn day. This cane against my clit feels incredible - until it moves away a couple inches, then returns in a swift stroke right between my thighs. The pain bursts across my pussy lips. I scream and try to close my legs, but he jams his foot between mine and prevents them from coming together.

"Keep your legs open," Ken growls.

His hand slides up, closes around my neck. His fingers hold me at my throat as he whips the cane back and forth between my thighs, catching my pussy over and over again with short little strokes which find my lips and clit and inner thighs. It's like being stung repeatedly by an angry hornet, and there is no escape from it because he has me by the throat and I can't breathe if I fight his grasp. The only way to keep getting oxygen is to keep my legs open and let him whip my cunt into a hot, sore, swollen state.

"You're mine," he growls, drawing me close, pushing the ridge of the cane against my tender pussy. "Don't ever fucking forget that, Mary. I don't care what happens in here. You're going to get out again, and you're going to be mine and I'm going to have you however I want."

He pushes me back and spins me around. The cane meets my ass in a hard cracking stroke. It burns like hell fire, and it's joined by another one almost immediately.

Six of the best is the usual dose of the cane. Ken gives me twelve. Twelve times that hard rod whips through the air and terminates across the fullest part of my ass. I am not going to sit for a very long time. I am not going to touch my pussy for a long time. He has turned my ass and cunt against me, the sensitive skin so impossibly sore I try to escape the cane's subsequent strokes by dropping to the ground, writhing in front of him as he follows me down and keeps applying pain.

"Don't you ever think about pulling this shit again," he growls in my ear as I lie on the floor, gasping for air.

"I won't, sir!" I cry the promise. The cold floor feels so good against my caned little clit. I roll over and face him, wailing as my ass meets the floor, but he holds me there anyway. Makes me feel every bit of it. His eyes sweep over me and find mine.

I am totally at his mercy. I feel that to my core. And

I don't ever want to cross him again. No matter what. The pain isn't worth it. I can see something else in his eyes. Determination. He didn't want to do this. But he will do it again if he has to.

We look at each other for a long moment. There's so much between us. So much unsaid. I want to beg him for just a little kindness. He wants to give it. But I just finished fucking him again and he won't, maybe can't. I've delayed his ability to love me again.

His hand slides between my legs. He rubs my slit briefly. It's hard to explain how it's not a sexual touch, even though it's on my genitals, but it isn't. It's one little moment of tenderness. One moment of connection. And it's all either of us are going to get.

"Get up and pull your pants up," he says as he slides his hand away. "You need to go see someone."

"W… who?"

"The woman you met at your intake. She runs this place. She wants to see you."

I whimper as I pull my pants back up. This is the sorest I've ever been. Actually, no, it's not. I've been in much worse pain before. This is the most pain I've ever allowed myself to feel. Because it came from him. And because I deserve it.

"That woman runs this place, sir?"

"Yeah," he says, tossing the cane on the bed. "And it was her car that you stole."

I sniff back the tears which are threatening to leak out of my eyes. She's going to fucking destroy me.

It's very, very hard to have any kind of composure after being caned like that. I want to hide under my blankets and never come out. But that's not how this works. When you fuck up to the level I just did, the consequences just keep coming.

As I enter her office, I feel her eyes on me. She's noticing how I'm walking. She probably knows exactly what Ken just did to me. I am sore and I am humiliated. Usually I'd be self-righteous about it, but somehow, when I look at this woman, I feel as though I deserve it.

The Head, as Ken calls her, is so composed. And she has a gravitas about her which makes me feel immediately small. Small, and messy and wrong.

"You wanted to see me, ma'am?" I address her respectfully. I do not want the consequences if I piss her off more. Everyone here is mad at me. An entire facility full of people were scrambled out of bed at three am because of my escape. I am not going to be popular for a long time.

"I want to show you something, Mary."

This woman always gets directly to the point. She makes no small talk. She does not bother with pleasantries, or excess communication. She has said only a few words to me so far, at the beginning of my stay, when she told me I was Ken's material. I am afraid of what she will say now.

I wipe my eyes and nod, waiting to see what it is. Something on her desk maybe. A file or something.

She walks over to me, stands in front of me, and lifts the bottom of the perfectly pressed blouse she's wearing, revealing the lower part of her tummy.

Her stomach is a scar. It runs dead across her belly button, and to one side, a big gnarled, old cross which must have been a nasty incision when it was made. I stare at it, shocked at the depth and the rawness of it. I would never have guessed a woman as elegant and poised as her could be hiding such a thing beneath her clothes.

"I know what it is to be kept and to be hurt," she says, her eyes locked on mine. "I know what it is to be an enemy of everyone and an ally of no-one. I know what it is to be entirely alone in the world. You are not alone anymore, Mary, and I can tell you two things for certain. Ares will not give up on you. Nor will I. But that doesn't mean your time here can't hurt a lot more than it needs to."

"It hurts a lot now," I say, ruefully. The cane marks are not going anywhere any time soon. I'm going to feel them for days. Even the most simple physical drills are going to feel like hell.

"It could always hurt more, couldn't it?"

I nod silently.

"I've been where you are now, Mary. I've stood where you're standing. Metaphorically. You have a choice to make. You can stay inside the world you've made for yourself, where you're safe, but ultimately alone - or you can come out and join the rest of us."

There's a silence. A space in which I think. I don't

entirely understand what she's saying, but I can sense it's important. I feel so stupid. I know there's something I'm missing. Something I've been missing since I've got here. But nobody seems to be able to explain it to me.

"I'm sorry I took your car," I say, filling the space between us with words. "It's just, it's the only one that can come and go without question. I watched it from the top windows a few times. Noticed that they never stop it. So…"

Her voice is calm, but cool as she replies. "If you touch a vehicle of mine again, I will make what Ares just did to you feel like a spa day in Zermatt, understand?"

"Yes, ma'am," I swallow.

She reaches out and puts a hand on my shoulder. "You have a future here, Mary. We do the things nobody else will do. We take on the people others don't want to take on. You will have the chance to face the people who hurt you one day. But not if you don't settle down and let the process work."

"I don't even know what I'm doing wrong," I admit. "I mean, aside from escaping. I keep failing, but I don't know how to succeed."

Her eyes soften a little.

There's compassion there.

For me.

"Let him do his job, Mary. You will understand soon enough."

KEN

"We're going to talk now."

She's back from the Head and she's tired. I can see it in her posture and in the dark circles under her eyes, and in the way she slumped down onto the mattress as soon as she got back here.

I was waiting for her, of course. I'm not done with her yet, not by a long way.

She shifts uncomfortably on the bed, looking guilty and sore. She's probably both. I really went in on her with that cane. Not that she didn't deserve it, but still. Intimate punishment of that nature deserves some kind of after care. In this situation, my ability to look after her is severely limited. I'll do what I can.

This process hasn't involved a lot of talking so far, and that's part of the problem. She's good with language, and I'm concerned if I engage her in a lot of talking, it will just take longer to train her because she'll talk me in circles. But after what she just did, some kind of conversation is absolutely in order.

"You stole a car."

"I needed one."

"Tom told me what you tried to do to Stephanie. Before I came home. Back at the house. With the lighter."

"Okay."

She looks at me under her lashes. She's still. Quiet. Holding it all in. Keeping her secrets locked as far away from me as possible. Dealing with Mary is like standing outside a high security vault. There are doors within doors within doors.

The only time I get to see her, the real her, is when she breaks down - and that hardly ever happens. Certainly hasn't since I bought her here. And I understand why. She's been taught to resist. If she can do one thing, it's lock the rest of the world out.

But I want in. I need in. And we don't have forever.

"Is there a point?" She looks at me and asks the question flatly.

"The point is, you do criminal things, Mary."

The corner of her lip flickers. "So?"

"So, most people feel guilty when they do things like that."

She looks at me blankly, and even though I know what I'm saying isn't reaching her, I don't know any other way to say it. I push through, hating that I have to rely on words. I'm not a man who speaks. I'm a man who does.

"And most people who were in your situation wouldn't run away from a place like this. Somewhere secure. Where certain foreign intelligences can't hurt them. Where they have a future."

"Most people aren't me," she shrugs.

"They're not," I agree. I want to know her. I have to know her. But I'll be fucked if I know the way in.

"What do you want, Ken?"

The directness of the question catches me off guard. She's looking me dead in the eye, and there's an intensity to her expression which makes me, a hardened soldier, suddenly feel a sinking sensation in the pit of my stomach. I've seen that look before. It's the look you see in the eyes of men who have done too much.

"I want you," I say, crouching down in front of her and taking her by the hand.

"You own me. I'm your material. You have me."

"I mean, I want what's in here." I press my hand to the space between her breasts, where her heart beats.

"You want in," she says softly. "You're looking for something more. But there's nothing inside me. There's nothing left. They took it. I'm hollow now."

There's an edge to her voice I haven't heard before. She's not sad. She's not angry. She's… vacant.

"I don't believe that."

"You're looking for something you can't find. Maybe that's because it doesn't exist."

"It exists, Mary. You're still here. With me."

"If you say so."

She turns her face away from mine, breaks eye contact. Breaks me. I've wanted nothing more than to save this girl since the moment her profile came across my desk, but now I'm wondering if she is right. Mary might have been lost before I found her. Maybe I didn't save her. Maybe I was too late. Maybe the woman lying in that bed was already gone.

There's definitely evidence to that effect. She has no impulse control. She does whatever makes the most sense to her in any given moment. She's not stupid, but she has no interest in the long term, because in her world, there is no long term. There is only the now.

If I'm right about that, she might always need me watching her, making sure she's under some form of effective control, because she's obviously not interested in, or maybe even capable of, controlling herself.

And then I feel something. Her fingers curl around mine. She's holding on to me. She can't look at me. She can't bear to show me who she really is, but there's definitely some part of her that's still here. Still wanting. Still needing. Still loving.

I have felt this woman wrapped around me, I have seen her soul when I look into her eyes. I have touched what I need to touch.

I take a deep breath and remind myself that the woman sitting in front of me right now is one who has had to face hell recently. When those agents walked in, a part of her walked out, took refuge at the back of her brain and left me with the faction of her which is about survival first.

"We have something," I remind her, my hand still between the soft swells of her breasts. "We've been together. Really together."

"It was all an act," she says, her voice husky. "You wanted to fuck me, so I fucked you. I don't know what love is, Ken. You should get out of here. Before I take you down with me."

An act? She's one of the most blunt people I've ever known.

"You're no actress, Mary."

"Bullshit," she laughs, cold. "All I do is act. I spend my life watching others. Then I do what they do. I was taught to emulate. I could be anything. Your little fuck toy, their assassin. Whatever. There's nothing inside me. It was taken a long time ago.

"Mary…"

She looks back at me. She can only see me when she's angry.

"I was raised to be a spy. I was born to lie. There's nothing…" she takes a halting breath. "People learn who they are when they're young. I learned who everyone else was. I never met me."

That I can believe. Sleeper agents live lies. Their lives are never their own. Everything they do is a cover for something else. So maybe she doesn't know what it's like to be authentically her. But I do think she knows who she is and what she wants.

I slide my hand down from her breasts to between her thighs. She draws a breath in, and the skin on her cheeks flushes red.

"You feel me here, Mary?"

She nods quickly, sucking her lower lip between her teeth. I squeeze lightly, knowing that it's going to hurt a little. My cane whipped her cunt well and truly. She lets out a little whimper and begins to squirm.

"Stay still," I admonish her sharply. She does as she's told, her eyes locked on mine. There she is. She's always present when we make love. Arousal brings her back from oblivion.

The thin clothing doesn't offer her pussy much protection. I begin stroking my finger up and down the length of her slit, just the pad of it. Maybe I've been wrong to avoid sexual contact in her training. I thought it would be unprofessional and a distraction, but now I'm seeing that it focuses her like nothing else.

I can feel her lips parting beneath the fabric of her leggings, and I draw the pad of my finger up to where the greedy bud of her clit is waiting, erect. She lets out a soft little moan as my fingertip works in a circle around it.

"Keep looking at me, Mary," I murmur softly.

Her eyes had drifted down to my hand between her thighs. At my command, she looks back up at me, meets my gaze.

"Good girl."

MARY

My clit aches and throbs as he plays with it. This is not pleasure. This is a punishment which feels good.

Ken's other hand spreads my thighs wide. He makes me open myself for him as he kneels there between my legs and strokes the very same part of me he just disciplined.

I know what he wants from me. He wants me to be his. He wants me to be normal, insofar as anyone in this line of work can be normal. But I can't meet even that dubious standard. I am missing so much of what it means to be human. He might be a warrior, but he was one who grew up in a loving family, with a big brother who looked out for him. He was a boy before he was a man.

I was never a girl. I was a thing. A tool. I was trained.

And now he has brought me here and he wants to train me too. I only function when I am being handled, that is the truth of the matter. And now he has taken over where the others left off.

Except they never did this to me. They never made me feel. They always tried to dull the feeling out of me. Self control, that was key. I have cried more in the last few months between Ken and Tom than I ever did in the first eighteen years of my life.

He pinches the fabric and skin over my clit just firmly enough to get my attention.

"Come back to me, Mary," he growls softly. "What were you thinking about?"

"I was thinking how I've always had a handler," I say. "Other people have mothers, fathers, teachers, and then when they grow up, they have lovers, husbands. I have none of those things."

"I have been your lover," he reminds me, giving my pussy another squeeze.

"You're the closest," I agree. "But now you're just another handler."

"I am not just another damn thing," he growls, rising up. He comes up, I go down, laying back against the bed as he looms over me. The hard lines of his face, the impassioned look in his eyes, I drink them all in. His hand has not left my pussy for a second. He is cupping it now, holding it possessively.

"You do need a handler," he says. "Without one, you're a vicious little animal."

I smirk, because he's right. And he's only seen a fraction of the things I've done, and the things I'm capable of.

"I'm going to be more, Mary. When we're done here, I'm going to be a lot more."

Promises promises. What do they mean? Nothing. This is what handlers do. They put a carrot on a stick and they dangle the promise of normality in front of you. There's never any going back though.

"You don't believe me," he says, his eyes searching my face as his fingers start to work my clit. I'm wet. My juices have been seeping since he started touching me and now his fingers have found the sore little bud that hides between my lower lips and they're working it roughly. "You know what?" He breathes against my neck as he strums my cunt. "You don't need to believe me. You just need to do as you're damn well told."

I let out a cry as he rubs me to orgasm. This isn't elegant. It's not romantic. But it is urgent and fierce and it is all about showing me what he can do to me. He can cane my pussy and then make me cum, because I am his. His material.

Impending climax forces thoughts from my mind. Makes me a wet, wanton little animal, writhing beneath her male. He watches me the whole time, his eyes never leaving my face. He wants to see me give in to orgasm. He wants to know the moment he forces my nervous system to overload.

I have no choice in giving him what he wants. He pinches my clit and I cum, bucking against his hand, clutching at the thin sheet of the bed, lifting my hips to him and grinding my wet hole with desperate motions as he gives me those few last precious touches which take me all the way and then leave me panting on the bed beneath him.

I've lost control. Again.

Ken taps my cunt and stands up, a smile on his face. "You're going to be just fine, Mary," he informs me. "Get some sleep."

13

KEN

"How is she?"

Tom still asks me that question every day. Every day I give the same answer.

"She's doing okay."

"When can she come home?"

That's the harder question to answer. When can she come home? When I'm sure there's nothing left inside her I don't know about. When I can be a hundred percent certain that I know every crevice of the girl. She hid a lot from me in plain sight, and though that was somewhat on me for not seeing, I still need to make sure that I have the kind of bond with her where she can't tolerate dishonesty.

I need to be able to tell her to walk to the back of a plane and jump out without a parachute, if I tell her to. Total obedience. Total submission. Total openness. It's a very big ask, especially for a woman who has the kind of history she does.

I'm breaking her. I'm making her show me everything. I'm stripping away everything that's superfluous, and I'm leaving her only with what she needs. I see the desire in her eyes. Against all odds, it's still strong even though I've given her so many reasons to hate me.

It also makes this so much harder. If she knew how much I wanted to hold her, kiss her, make love to her, none of this would work. I have to be the ultimate authority. I have to be the one boundary she can never shift, no matter how much she tries. I have to be the circumference of her world.

Every night I have to put her into a little cell and go and lie in a different room and wish she was in my arms. This is hard on both of us, but I can't afford to show her that. She has to think that this is what I want from her. She has to give in, completely. She has to surrender.

MARY

"You're having a hard time, aren't you."

It's not a question. It's a statement of fact. And it's coming from a woman who is in a position to know.

I now have regular meetings with the Head. She seems to think I need some kind of personal care, or maybe it's just that I got her attention when I broke out of her facility and stole her car. I kind of get the impression she likes me, though I don't know why.

"A harder time than most people?"

"You're yet to pass your first assessment," she says. "Usually that happens in the first couple of days."

"Well, I guess I suck."

I am sitting on the window sill of her office. It looks out over the forest which surrounds the facility. These meetings are one of the few times in the week I get to see natural sunlight.

She is wearing a gray pantsuit. Her hair is tied back and rolled into a tight bun. In contrast to her formal attire and appearance, I am wearing a dark tracksuit and sneakers. My hair is getting longer now, so I tie it back in a ponytail.

"You don't 'suck'," she says. "You don't understand the lesson being taught."

"Well why don't you tell me what it is?"

"Ares is your handler," she says, telling me what I already know. "And he has been more than that to you in the past."

"Uh huh."

"There is a bond between handler and agent," the Head says. "A bond of trust and obedience."

"Okay, well I'll do what he says."

"And the first part?" She raises a brow and sips at her coffee.

"Trust him? I mean I have to."

"That's not trust."

I look over at her and sigh. "Well, what is trust then?"

"It's a skill you need to learn."

225

"That's not an answer."

"It is an answer. It's just not one you wanted to hear," she replies.

"So how much longer are you going to put up with me being the slowest kid on campus?" I change the subject.

"This takes as long as it needs to take," she replies calmly.

I know most people in her position aren't this patient. It costs money to keep me here. It costs money to pay Ken too. And getting him reassigned would have had a cost too, even if it wasn't monetary. This woman wants me here.

"What are you thinking?"

"I'm just wondering why you're being patient with me."

"You saw the reason," she says. "You're not the first person to find herself unexpectedly hospitalized. You're one of the very few to have survived it."

So that's what we have in common. Survival.

"It changes you, Mary. I know it does. And the circumstances around being raised as a spy, they change you too. Ares understands that."

"I don't think he understands anything about me," I mumble.

"No?"

"He's so distant now. And angry. I broke his trust. I don't think he can trust me again. Forget about me trusting him."

"Let me tell you how much he trusts you, Brown,"

226

she says, putting her cup to the side. "He trusts you enough that instead of handing you directly over to the authorities, he brought you to my attention. He put his professional and personal life on the line to bring you here. That's trust."

"And I repaid him by breaking out and failing every assessment since I got here…" I shake my head and put my face in my hands. "You're all wasting your time. You should put a bullet in me."

"If I thought that was necessary, it would already have been done."

I look over at her and see that she's serious. This woman truly has the power of life and death over me. I should be way more afraid of her than I am.

I wonder why I'm not.

And then it occurs to me. It's because I know Ken's here. Even if he's not in the room with me, I know he won't let me be hurt again.

Maybe I do trust him. Even if I do, I don't know how to act that trust out in a way these people can understand. I know they're waiting for me to do something, I just don't know what.

There is something else on my mind too. A question which has been with me since she showed me her scar. It's not polite to ask people too many questions about their life changing injuries, but I just have to know.

"Ma'am?"

"Yes?"

"The scar you showed me the other day…"

"Yes…"

"Did you ever get revenge on the people who did that to you?"

She takes another sip of coffee and I sit there, hoping I haven't offended her too badly.

"You've heard the saying the best revenge is living well?"

"Yeah."

Her silver eyes sparkle. "In our case, my dear, the best revenge is living at all."

KEN

"Ow goddamn!"

Mary curses under her breath as she struggles to maintain position. I can see she's on the verge of losing her temper. I've had her in a stress position sitting back against the wall with her arms outstretched for the last half an hour. Her legs are shaking, and her arms are, too. The lactic acid build up must be painful by now. She'll have trouble walking easily after this.

The truth of the matter is, I don't know how much longer I can keep this up. No matter what I do, she's just not breaking. She does what she's asked to do. She does it as best as she can. And ordinarily, that would be enough, but it's not where she's concerned.

I've lectured her. I've punished her. I've put her through physical training and mental exercises designed to exhaust her. She's come through every one of them the same.

The worst part of it is, she doesn't understand why this is happening. She thinks if she's just a good enough girl, this will all be over. But that's not the game we're playing.

Oversight has assessed her every week since she came in. They say she's still not ready. They're right. Years of being raised in a home by a Russian sleeper agent has fractured her mind. It's not that she's crazy. It's that she's compartmentalized. She keeps the demons all neatly locked away. She keeps her loyalties to herself. Her thoughts are hidden. She's an enigma, but like the code, she will be cracked.

Soon her arms waver, then fall to her sides.

"Back up."

She sits there, looking at her knees, and then she shakes her head. She follows the physical refusal with a soft word.

"No."

There it is. The rebellion I've been waiting for. A proper rebellion. Not a test. Not a game. She's losing her temper. The facade she always has at the ready is finally slipping.

She's been a good girl in training lately, and that has been a problem, because I know all too damn well that Mary is not a good girl at all. She is a very, very bad little girl, but she's been trying to hide that side from me behind a veneer of control. She doesn't get to have control anymore. I do.

"What was that?"

She pushes up from the wall and faces me. She's damn beautiful when she's angry.

"I said no."

"You don't have the option to say no."

"No! No! No! No!"

She yells the refusal at me. That spirit of hers is damn near indomitable, but I'm getting close now because finally she's actually losing control. She doesn't want to be shouting and screaming like a little girl. She wants to show me she can take this. But she can't. Of course she can't. Nobody can. That's the point.

"Get back into position," I demand.

"No!" She yells at me, her fists clenched. "I won't goddamn well do it!"

She comes for me, swinging her right arm. It's a feint and I see it immediately because the other fist is following up properly. I catch both hands and send her tumbling onto her butt, then stand over her, looking down at her furious little form.

"You want to fight me, Mary?"

MARY

Yes, I want to fight him.

I want to kick his viciously handsome, totally sadistic ass. For weeks I've been trying to please him, but nothing does. It's obvious he's never going to forgive me. He's just going to keep on hurting me, putting me through stupid pointless training that doesn't teach me a damn thing.

I know I don't have a chance in hell of actually beating him. He outweighs me, outranks me, and can definitely outfight me. But I want to hit him so fucking bad I'm willing to risk what inevitably comes next. Maybe jail for the rest of my life. Maybe a beating. Maybe solitary. I don't know, and I don't fucking care.

"Fuck you, Ken," I swear. "You can go to fucking hell. I'm going to fail no matter fucking what. The Head is wrong. You don't want me. This is just your fucked up way of getting revenge on me because you didn't know I was a spy. Well, maybe that's your fucking fault!"

He says nothing. Just stares at me and crooks a finger at me in a plain invitation to come at him. He's not concerned in the slightest. He knows I'm in the middle of making a mistake, and he's not going to stop me.

I wish I could stop me, but the rage I've been burying for years is bursting free. All the anger I've had at being held captive, experimented on, hurt, lied to. All the fury at being forced to lie to everyone I know, never, ever being able to relax and enjoy my life, bursts out of me in a feral scream.

I throw myself at him using everything at my disposal. Fists. Knees. Elbows. Teeth. I let my rage out on him in a vicious display unlike any I have allowed myself before. The asshole in Afghanistan got off light compared to Ken.

Unlike that man, Ken is able to withstand my assault. I don't even make direct contact with his body before he deflects my blows and hems me up in a grip that makes it impossible to move. I am held on the floor, seething with naked rage.

"If you don't want me anymore, just fucking kill me!"

"Absolutely not, little girl," he growls in my ear. He hasn't called me little girl in a very long time. Hearing it now jolts me back into a time when he was my lover, my rescuer, my friend. I would give anything to get back to that, if only I knew what I needed to do.

KEN

Now. Something inside my head says. *Do it now.*

Keeping her firmly under control, I crouch on the floor, one leg up in basically a proposal position. Instead of asking this squirming little wench to marry me, I sweep her over my knee. Her perfect ass is presented to me and I start spanking it hard with the flat of my palm.

When she came here she took her rebellion and her rage and she locked it all away to try and keep it secret from me. The more I took away from her, the more she retreated into a shell of what she thought I wanted. There have been moments of truth, but they weren't like this. They were calculated misbehaviors of the kind that needed to be put down with sterile discipline, cold and detached. It served a purpose, but now it's time for something more. Something we've both been craving for a long time.

"I was trying to be good!" Her wail is plaintive and confused.

She's wearing lycra training clothes that don't give fuck all protection, but having her train naked was starting to raise a few brows. I explained that I wanted complete access to every part of her, and this was the compromise we came up with. A bodysuit which hugs her sexy curves - and which tears at a rough grasp. After a few dozen hard slaps, I yank the fabric off her butt, tearing a hole in the seat of the suit, and I spank her bare cheeks hard and fast, making her wail like the little girl she hasn't been allowed to be.

She doesn't understand why I'm doing this, because this isn't fair. It can't be fair either, and it can't be explained. She has to go through it to really understand it.

"You're mine, Mary. You can't hide any part of yourself from me. You have to show me everything. Tell me everything. When something hurts, I want to see it. You can have your facade for the world. You can be stoic and shield yourself against pain for other people. For me, you show me everything. Including the things you think I don't want to see."

"You want me to be undisciplined? I don't get it!" She shrieks. "I've been trying so fucking hard, Ken."

"It's always a facade with you when you try. You put on a new identity and you wear it. You thought you were doing as you were told, but you were just hiding from me again."

"So how the fuck do I win?" She gasps as my hand whips her cheeks, turning them from pink to red.

"That's the point," I say. "You don't win. You stop trying to win. You stop trying to control by being good or bad. You accept what's coming to you. That's the difference between real obedience and what you've been giving me."

"Oh."

I feel the moment she gets it. Her whole body relaxes. She surrenders. Properly, and probably for the very first time in her life.

This is now truly my girl over my knee.

She lays there as I swat her a few more times, and then rub her cheeks. It might seem like a minor moment to an outsider, but to me, this is everything. This is the holy grail.

"Good girl," I murmur soothingly, patting and rubbing her cheeks. She has a gorgeous ass. Not being able to play with it or fuck it has been absolute torture.

I want her so fucking badly. I have been so damn patient, but I can't be anymore. She finally surrendered. She gave me what I wanted her to give. And now I'm going to take the rest.

I drop my knee and let her red-bottomed body slide to the floor. She lies there, her legs spread, her pussy visible through the tear in her pants. She's wet. I can smell her. It's driving me mad with need as I unbuckle my pants and free my cock.

Once she tried to tempt me with this, tried to wrest control of the situation. Now she's abandoned all hope of control and she lies there in wet, willing submission.

This is not part of official protocol, but fuck it. She's mine, dammit. She's always been mine. I caned this naughty little cunt not that long ago. I couldn't have taken her then. It would have been too close to a hate fuck, but I don't hate her. I love her. I love her to the point I will whip her pussy if I have to. There's no need to punish her anymore though. She's been a good girl. A very good girl. And it's time she felt that.

"Ken…" I hear her soft voice as I put my hand to her ass, cup her bright red cheeks and slide two fingers into the wet furred slit between them.

"You want this, Mary?"

I haven't used her first name in almost two months. It feels strange on my tongue. It feels even stranger to ask her if she wants this. It's the first choice I've given her in that same period of time.

"Please…" she lifts her hips and rolls them in a way that can only signify assent.

I pull my fingers free, get between her thighs, wrap my fist around my cock and slide between her lower lips. The second my cock touches her sex, I feel how fucking soaked she is. I'm titanium hard. Not getting laid for two months will do that.

Reaching down, I grab a handful of her hair and pull her head back, feeding my cock into her tight pussy in a devastatingly slow stroke which lets me feel every bit of her sweet cunt.

She's tight and slick, and her inner walls grip me

with all the desperation of a long lost lover. It's an incredible feeling, to be enveloped by her body, to feel her tight heat, her eager wetness. This is the only place on Earth I want to be. This is all I've wanted for weeks. It was worth the wait.

"I missed you so fucking much," I growl as I slowly sink my cock all the way to the hilt.

MARY

He's fucking me. I'm fucking him. Did I do something right? Or something wrong? I don't even know. I gave up. I know that much. I gave up trying to control what became of me and in that same moment, he came to me hard and fast and he swept me off my feet and now he is stretching my pussy wide.

I can feel my breasts pressed against the cool floor, my clit exposed by the ragged tear in my suit to grind against the hard surface.

His words make my pussy clench. Tears mist my eyes. I missed him so fucking much. Every night I wished he was with me. Every time we were together it was all I could do not to throw myself at his feet and just beg for forgiveness.

And now I'm on the floor, my cunt sliding in my own juices as he fucks me against the ground, his hard hips slapping my already punished ass with hard strokes.

This is rough and primal. His arm snakes around under my neck and he holds me in position, sinking his thick cock inside me over and over again. Somehow every time it goes in, it feels even bigger and harder than it did the time before.

He shouldn't be doing this. But he is, and I can feel the reason. Because he can't wait another fucking minute for me, just like I couldn't stand another second without him.

We make frantic, passionate love, the kind where the only thing that matters is that he is inside me. He pulls out, flips me onto my back and thrusts inside me all over again, his hands wrapped in my hair, his mouth on mine.

"Forgive me," I moan between thrusts.

"You're forgiven," he growls. "You're so fucking forgiven."

He hikes my legs up around his waist and I wrap them around him, clinging to him as he pounds me. We kiss, embrace, grind, we are lost to everything but one another until orgasm frees us and leaves us lying spent on the floor.

"ARES!"

A voice comes over the speaker I didn't know was in the room. Ken lets out a little groan and helps me to stand, tucking his cock away once I'm on my feet.

"YOU BETTER GET THAT FLOOR MOPPED!"

We look at each other, and I do the other thing I haven't done in two months: I laugh.

"Shit," he says. "I'm going to get some heat for that. Worth it though."

He pulls me tight against his body and I sink into

his embrace, feel his strength. I hear the beating of his heart. I thought he'd abandoned me emotionally, but he never went anywhere. He stayed right by my side and he did what needed to be done, even though I hated him for it.

I lean my head against his shoulder. "I am so sorry," I murmur. "I've ruined everything for you."

"You've ruined nothing," he says gruffly. "You needed what you needed."

"I needed to be locked up and chased around with a cane naked for two months?"

"You needed to be broken down," he says, his arms cradling me close, one hand sliding down over my hip to rub my hot, bare ass. "So we can build you up. Real trust this time. Real truth. No lies. Nothing hidden."

"Nothing hidden," I repeat, feeling lighter than ever before. It's true, I realize. There is now nothing hidden between us. I have shown him my scars, my sadness, my hate, my fear. He has seen it all and it has not changed a thing. He is here for me, guiding me, disciplining me, making me the best I can be.

"I love you," I say. "Even if I hate you sometimes."

He smiles down at me. "Oh I'm sure you'll continue to hate me sometimes," he says. "But at least now you'll know that I love you too."

KEN

It's taken months to get her to this point. It's been hard won, but it's worth it. Now it's time to release the pressure on both of us. It's also time to make ourselves presentable for the walk of shame we're about to do when we leave this room. Her ass is still displayed gorgeously red in the torn suit, but I don't intend on rectifying that issue just yet.

"You understand what just happened, Mary?"

She nods, tears in her eyes. "I think so."

"You don't need to hide anything from me," I repeat. "Past. Present. Future. There's nothing I don't want to know about you. There's nothing I don't want to see."

"So this hasn't just been about you hating me and punishing me?"

"No. This has been about breaking down some of those walls you have in your mind, Mary." I tap her forehead gently. "It's been about getting inside you. The real you."

"So is my training over?" She looks into my eyes with a hopeful gaze.

"Oh no, sweetheart. This is where your training starts."

Her face falls. "I'm never going home, am I?"

"Wrong again," I say, using my fingers to tip her face up toward me. "We're going home today."

Her expression brightens adorably. In this moment, she is happier than she has been in a very long time. "We are?"

Damn straight we are. I'm reinforcing that perfect surrender with the only currency she cares about: being home with her daddy and me. We are everything to her, and she is everything to us.

The road ahead is long, and dangerous. She's got a lot to learn. I have a lot of work to do. But I can finally look into her eyes and see her there. Not the Mary she fabricated to get by in the world, but the real Mary, the Mary I can build up, the Mary I can love. The Mary I will have forever.

"Come on," I say. "Let's get you cleaned up and ready to get out of here."

"Yes, sir."

The *sir* comes so easily to her now. She used to whimper it at first. Then she would only growl it. Now it comes in a grateful, swift response. I should have better control of myself, but after what we just did I can't help the impulse to sweep her into my arms and kiss her thoroughly, our lips meeting, parting, tongues twirling with the need we have been holding back for far too long.

She's mine. All mine. I own her body and soul. I should have hunted her little ass down after she was evacuated from Chile. I could have saved us both so much suffering. But what's done is done. We have both made mistakes. We both have so much work to do. And I don't know if we'll survive what the future holds, but I know I finally have her. All of her. And that's all I've ever wanted.

14

MARY

"Time to get to work."

Those words make me nervous.

This is our first assignment and I'm terrified that I am going to fuck it up. I've never carried out a successful mission in my life. We've been contracted to deal with some people smuggling drug runners. Relatively small time. I know this is basically a test. They want to see if I'm actually useful. I'm fairly certain I won't be.

Because this is so small time, it's just Ken and I. Our mission is simple enough. Go in and take the leader captive. He'll be either broken or traded or god knows what. That's not our concern.

Ken will do all the heavy lifting. All I have to do is stay in the rear and not fuck up. Should be easy enough.

We're not even going all that far. We're not leaving the state. This is a short, hop, skip and a jump to a part of the countryside where some people with very bad intentions have set themselves up to supply people who should know better.

"You stay on my six," he says. "Any sign of trouble, you take cover. This is a small operation, we're not expecting much resistance, but you never know."

He's fucking hot in this mode, but I can't allow myself to be distracted. This is real. And I have to prove myself. Specifically, I have to prove that I'm not a total loose cannon, that I can follow orders and that I can be trusted in the field. Even I don't know if any of those things are true. I guess we're about to find out.

It takes way too fucking long to hike to the spot. We're dropped off several miles away and we have to walk in. These guys like it remote.

There's no talking though. There's just three hours of Ken's ass moving in perfect concert inside black tactical pants. I'm fucking hungry for this man. When this is over, I'm going to devour him.

It's probably not normal to be horny as hell heading into a mission, or maybe it is. Arousal, fear, excitement, they're all basically the same thing. This is a slow burn of anticipation. As soon as we get our man, we'll be choppered out. And later on tonight, I've been promised a celebration.

Today is a good day.

Until everything goes wrong.

Good things take time. Bad things happen instantly.

We are still ten minutes out from the target when a blast of smoke and sound disorients me. Flash grenade. Thrown right the fuck at us.

There's shouting. It might be mine. It might be Ken's. I don't know what the hell is happening. I can't see and I can't hear. Fumbling about in the fog, I grab for the nearest thing that feels human. It takes hold of me, wraps around me.

THUNK

Something hard and heavy smacks me over the skull. My world goes dark.

———

When I come to, they have me. One of my eyes is swollen. I spit dried blood out of my mouth. A tooth goes with it. Left canine, by the looks of things.

I'm not tied up. That's… interesting. I sit up, look down with my one good eye, and see that I've been laid out on a stained mattress. My vest has been taken off. My shirt is partially open. Not a good sign. But my belt is still on. I guess they didn't like what they saw when they pulled my bra down.

"What the fuck happened to you?"

The question is spat at me by a man sitting at a table across the room. The twisted up look on his face says it all. His disgust saved me from a brutal assault. Never thought I'd be glad to be missing a nipple.

"Some limp dick pussy tried to fuck me, I think," I say, taunting him on purpose.

The thing about men who are used to hurting women is that they forget that not everyone is their victim. This guy is wearing a knife and a gun on his waist, making himself a walking weapon rack.

It takes him a full thirty seconds to realize I'm talking about him. The realization dawns slower than grass grows. So he's sloppy *and* stupid. Awesome.

"What did you just say to me, you ugly whore?" He comes storming over, like the fucking idiot he is. In a split second, the knife which was at his waist is in my hand. The point is in his brachial artery.

He's not quite dead by the time he hits the floor, but in another twenty seconds he will be. I don't have time to listen to the whimpering and the gurgling. I have to find Ken.

This shack has a basement, and there are unpleasant sounds coming from it. I work my way slowly down the stairs, knife in hand, to see what's going on.

Ken is tied up against the wall, Jesus style. A-fuck-ing-men. Three men are interrogating him, mostly by yelling at him and hitting him repeatedly with a piece of wood. Simple, but probably effective enough over time. He's going to be a mass of bruises.

I walk up to the middle man and shove the knife between his ribs from the back. He's dead before the other two even realize it. They don't notice anything is wrong until I push him forward and off the blade. There's an almost comical moment where their comrade keels over face first, and they suddenly realize that there's a problem.

Me.

The first man to turn toward me meets the point of my knife in different fashion, right across the belly, clean and smooth. His insides become his outsides in spectacularly short order, a cascade of viscera making a mess of all our shoes.

There's one man left. I turn toward him, knife ready to remove soul from flesh.

He throws up and passes out.

It's well played. Even I don't kill unconscious people. Isn't sporting.

I leave him in his vomit and turn my attention to the task of getting Ken out of here.

He hasn't made a sound since I came into the room, although, to be fair, it's only been sixty seconds since I started killing.

"I didn't teach you to do that," he says from his spreadeagled place on the wall.

"I know," I say, as I work on the bonds on hands. "They did."

"Who did?"

"The hospital," I say. "They made me watch things. When you watch, you learn."

"I never thought I'd be glad you were ever in there," he says. "And I'm still not, but... goddamn."

"You made me faster at it," I say conversationally. "Would have taken me longer if it had happened before you trained me."

"Huh."

He slides gingerly down from the wall, rubbing his

wrists and looking at me with an expression I know signals the end of our love.

Now he's seen it all. The part of me I tried my best to hide. The capacity no good woman is ever supposed to have. He always knew I was a monster, I think. But now he knows it for absolute certain. It's easy to feel sorry for me and look past the scars. Fucking a charity case is one thing. But wanting a woman who just did what I did? Not going to happen. Women function as repositories of goodness for bad men. That's how it always is.

"Sorry I fucked this up."

"You didn't," he says. "That guy on the floor is the one we want. Let's get him out of here."

He bends down to grab the guy, but doesn't get more than an inch or so bent before he curses and straightens with a gasp.

"I've got him," I say, laying hands to his boots. I start dragging the asshole out feet first. Ken follows, armed and watchful, calling in the cavalry.

———

Our extraction team is not too far away. I guess the Head figured we might need it. The helicopter swoops in like a dark angel, picks us up and within five minutes, it's like we were never there.

The helicopter is loud. It's impossible to have a conversation between the rapid beating of the blades. Instead, Ken just holds my bloodied hand.

The moment we land inside our compound, others take over. The poor bastard in the back is about to have a very, very bad day.

Ken is sore. He needs medical attention. I tell him as much, and hear the last thing I ever wanted to hear.

"You need to see the doctor too."

"Nope."

"No doctor," I insist.

"We have a new one on staff. I think you'll like him."

"There's only one doctor I'd ever see and…" I trail off as Ken's lips twist into a knowing smirk. "You got Tom hired here too?"

"He's a military surgeon whose ex-wife ruined his civilian career. He'll do well here," Ken shrugs. "And you're going to see him, if I have to pick you up and drag you to him."

"You couldn't pick up a kitten right now," I point out.

Ken lets out a growl and advances on me, keen to prove me wrong. Before he can hurt himself macho-ing out on me, I raise my hands in surrender. "Okay! Okay! Fine!"

15

_____

MARY

It's damn good to see Tom again. I don't think it's as good for him to see me. As I come through the door, he pales. His jaw clenches. When an Ares man is angry, it's an impressive thing to behold. Tom has a good grip on his temper though, and he manages to hold it together.

"What the hell happened to her?" He crosses the room over to me and half-crouches in front of me. "Mary…"

"I'm fine," I say, stepping back before he can start gushing all over me. "Do Ken first. He's actually broken. I'm just bruised."

"Come over here and…"

"No," I pull back again. Tom's not getting it. "Ken first."

I'd be telling Ken to go first even if my head was hanging off. I trust Tom, but medical stuff will never not creep me out. And he really does need the treatment first.

"I'll go first," Ken agrees. "Show you there's nothing to be scared of."

There's plenty to be scared of, but not with Tom around. He examines Ken competently, puts him through an x-ray, and comes to much the same conclusion I did - broken ribs.

"You're going to have to take it easy," he says. "Off active duty for eight weeks at least."

"Oh come on," Ken grunts. "Ribs take six weeks to heal."

"Eight weeks," Tom insists. "Keep talking and I'll make it twelve."

I snort with amusement. Tom almost never gets all dominant with Ken, but in doctor mode, he's definitely in charge. That makes me all the more nervous when it comes to be my turn.

"Alright you, up on the table," he says, slapping the white papered surface.

I get up there against my better judgement. All I need is a painkiller and a hot towel to clean off with.

Tom starts with the cleaning, using warm water and a bit of saline.

"I know it hurts," he says sympathetically as I try not to flinch. They really fucking caught me across the face. Tooth. Nose. Eye. All up the fuck. But it could be a lot worse.

Cleaning all the blood and stuff off takes a while.

He works carefully and gently, taking care of me as best he can.

"I'm sorry," I mumble.

"Sorry for what?"

"Sorry you have to see me like this. I know I look all fucked up."

"Don't apologize for that," he says grimly.

"It's worse than it looks," I say.

It's true. It looks messy, but I've had far worse. The pain is going to kick in soon, but I'm pretty sure he's going to give me decent enough pain relief to deal with that. Right now, I'm still running on adrenaline and I feel bulletproof.

"Settle down, little girl," he says as I squirm under his hands.

"I'm not a little girl," I protest. "I just killed four men with my bare hands."

"I don't care how many men you killed," he says patiently. "Sit still for me while I take your blood pressure."

"You don't care?" I look at him under my lashes as he fits the cuff on my arm.

"I was in the military too," he reminds me. "I know what happens."

What we just did wasn't the sort of thing they do in the military, I don't think. Or maybe it is. I don't know. I've never been in. It's what I do to survive though, and I guess that's similar enough.

"I think you're alright," he says finally. "You're going to need to see a dentist for that tooth… other than that,

I'm not seeing anything of medical concern. You're bruised, but everything is intact."

"See? I'm fine."

"Mhm," Ken rumbles.

KEN

She really is pretty damn close to being fine. She's missing a tooth and now she's cleaned up a bit, she somehow manages to look almost cute with the little gap which we'll have to have fixed just as soon as we find enough rope to tie her down for a dentist to see her.

I am unspeakably proud of her in this moment. The first mission is always difficult. The first mission going wrong is very bad news. We have no business being alive. And we wouldn't be, if it wasn't for her.

In that basement, she was a whirlwind of death. Those poor bastards never had a chance. When it comes to killing, technique and practice are key, but they're nothing if you don't have the inner steel to do it. She does.

She's absolutely dangerous. She always will be. She's a weapon and in the wrong hands she could do untold damage. But she's mine.

I don't like seeing her hurt. I could have fucking burst with rage when she came in streaming blood. But now, I don't know. Something is different. I'm starting to realize she's in her element. Brutality suits her.

The life she's led has taken a lot from her, but it's

made her tough as hell in other ways. She's sitting there with a half smile, and I'm watching Tom try to wrangle her into taking a shot. We all know she'll let him in the end. This is just her way of making sure he's still in charge.

"Ares. Head wants to see you."

A summons from the Head cannot be ignored. I make my way gingerly to the woman's office, thoroughly expecting to be chewed out for the shit show which just ensued.

———

"You wanted to see me, ma'am?"

"Congratulations, Ares."

I literally never know what this woman is going to say. She's unpredictable as all hell.

"Thank you, ma'am."

"Mary is cleared for full status," she says. "You can tell her the good news."

"Thank you, ma'am."

"That's all."

But that's not all. It can't be all. She's not even going to mention that we were both almost taken captive? That doesn't make sense to me. This woman rules with an iron fist. I'm pretty damn certain she doesn't approve of mistakes. And a huge mistake was made today.

"Ma'am, a question?"

"Yes, Ares?" She looks up from the documents on

her desk, and I feel the full force of being an inconvenience.

"Why wasn't there backup?"

The Head looks at me with those steel gray eyes of hers. "You didn't need it."

"We needed it."

"No," she disagrees. "That girl needed to know she's capable of surviving.

I have been racking my brain since we got clear how they knew we were there. Our approach was practically flawless. We tripped no wires, the security was laid out in the schematics and we flanked all of it. But they were waiting for us when we walked in. Like they had nothing better to do than just sit there and… holy shit.

"You…." I draw in a breath. "You tipped them off on purpose."

"They were rogue operatives from another branch. Scheduled for destruction. No loss."

Jesus Fucking Christ. This woman.

"You could have lost us," I point out.

"If we'd have lost you, you wouldn't have been worth having." She gives me one of those thin, tight smiles. "You need to work on your reaction time, Ares. You were slow. You're lucky she was there."

"Yes," I say through gritted teeth. "I guess I was. But ma'am…"

"Yes, Ares?" She raises her chin, as if daring me to say what she knows I'm going to say.

"If you ever put us in a situation with bad intel again, I'll tell Mary."

The Head breaks into a genuine smile. "Ah, you know how to make a threat, don't you. Never fear, Ares. The testing period is over. Any damage you take from here on out will be entirely organic. I give you my word."

16

MARY

Tom will not stop fussing over me.

"I'm fine," I insist.

"You have contusions all over your head," he scowls at me. "When I get you home, you're going straight into the bath, little girl, and then to bed."

"I am a stone cold killer," I remind him. "Assassins don't have bed times."

"This one does," Tom rumbles. "And she has a daddy to make sure she gets there on time too. Ken is going to be out of commission for a little while. So you're going to be answering to me at home."

"Boring," I pout, even though I am secretly thrilled. I need home. I need comfort. I need to feel just a little domestic. It's not that I feel bad for what I did today. It's that sometimes, the fact that I don't feel bad scares me. Tom is my one connection to the world of typical humans. When I'm with him, I feel like I have some access to the realm of the ordinary.

Tom's arms wrap around me. He pulls me onto his lap and cuddles me right there in the doctor's office. I snuggle into his embrace and rest my head on his chest. This is more therapeutic than a thousand painkillers and stitches.

"Ken's not going to want me anymore," I say softly.

"What?"

"He saw me do those things today," I mumble, my fingers playing with Tom's shirt. "He won't like me after that."

"I guarantee you Ken has seen worse."

"Yeah, but he hasn't seen his girlfriend do it."

"You looked phenomenal."

Ken must have heard the tail end of the conversation as he came in the door.

"What are you talking about, Mary?"

Shit. Hearing him say my name sends a tremor right through to the core of me.

"Nothing," I mumble.

"Tell him, little girl," Tom prompts me.

"Yes, tell me, little girl," Ken echoes.

I am trapped between two Ares men with no way out. Surrender is the only option, even though it involves confessing my biggest fear for a second time.

I avoid Ken's gaze as I repeat what I said to Tom in a mumble. "I know you don't want to be with me now."

"What?"

"You don't want to…"

"I heard what you said," Ken interrupts me, incredulous. "How could you possibly think that?"

"I mean, you saw... what I did."

"Your job?" He shifts uncomfortably and grimaces to let me know it's not because of me. Broken ribs hurt like a bitch, and there's basically nothing anybody can do. "Girl, I could watch that all day."

"But... it was... I was..." I mime stabbing and blood spurting with splayed fingers.

He frowns and tries to cross his arms over his chest, only to remember that hurts like hell, and put them back by his side.

"You saved both our lives," he rumbles. "You saved yourself. And me. And you did it quick and clean. You didn't do anything wrong, Mary. You were perfect."

"I was?"

Tom rubs my back as Ken reassures me from his uncomfortably stiff position.

"You were everything I needed you to be. You understand that? Those men needed to die. They were going to kill us both. You did what you should have done. Hell, you did what I should have done. I should be apologizing to you. Don't..." his voice breaks just a little. "Don't ever think I don't want you."

Tom's arms snug around me, giving me the hug I know Ken would if it didn't risk puncturing his lung with a shard of shattered rib.

Suddenly I understand something I think I've known from the first time our eyes met in that fucked up hospital. Ken is just like me. He's my soulmate. He understands me. There is no part of me, no thought, no fear, no scar, that could change his love for me. And there is absolutely nothing that could change my love for him.

Hot tears run down my face. They hurt, coming from one sore and swollen eye and one good one, but they are tears of joy which is bursting through my body. I am loved. I am loved to the very core of me. And no matter what happens in life, that will always be true.

EPILOGUE: TOM

"Little girl, where are you!?"

"I'm hiding," the curtains declare.

Months of training and she still doesn't seem to realize that her sneakers can clearly be seen sticking out from under the curtains. Or maybe she does. She only plays around like this when Ken's not here. He doesn't find it as funny as I do, or as cute.

"Well, I guess I'll have to eat these cookies on my own," I say, sitting down on the couch with the tray in front of me.

I take a cookie and start eating. Approximately two seconds later, I hear a voice at my ear. "Give me the cookies and I won't sell your secrets, mister."

I reach back, grab her by the back of her jersey, and flip my little spy over the couch and onto the seat next to me in a forward somersault which she executes perfectly. She's more adept than she likes to make out.

Ken's training has produced some real changes in her. She's fitter, faster… and happier.

"Zees cookies are mine!" She declares, grabbing three of them.

"Mary, put them down. You can have one," I censure her.

"You drive a hard bargain, mister," she mumbles, relinquishing the excess.

"Mhm."

EPILOGUE: KEN

I don't know why, but I'm always the one on the beer runs. Hardly seems fair, especially when I come back home to discover that Tom and Mary have put a hell of a dent in the cookie stash.

"Are those chocolate chip?"

"Yesssir. I've conducted intense surveillance, and I can assure you that they're chocolate chip, they're delicious and..." she pops the last piece in her mouth. "They're all gone."

"Brown!" I snap her work name at her and watch her pale a little. Good. Nice to see she doesn't completely forget who is in charge even when Tom spoils her silly.

"Whaffat, fur?" Her question is muffled thanks to the ungodly amount of cookie in her mouth.

"Get over here," I growl, putting the beer down and pointing at the floor in front of me.

She vaults over the couch and comes to me double

quick, looking up at me ready to receive instructions. Oh she's trained alright. Like a naughty Golden Labrador. I reach out with my thumb and brush a few stray crumbs off her cheek.

"I love you, brat," I say with a smile.

She smiles back broadly. "I love you too, sir."

The *sir* really has become a habit with her. I don't mind it one bit either. Smiling, I hand her a beer. "Go give that to your daddy."

"Sir, yessir!" She salutes and runs the beer over to him, knees high, double time. God, she is incorrigible.

It's hard to believe she was ever that pale waif so horribly hurt in that hospital bed. It's harder still to believe that she was a foreign agent trapped in a web of lies. What's not hard to believe is that she's mine. I went to the gates of hell for this girl, and that was only the beginning. I'd do anything for her. I will be whatever she needs be to be. Her lover. Her handler. One day very soon, her husband.

EPILOGUE: MARY

The cookies are good. Ken is better.

He saved me.

He saved me from hell.

He saved me from myself.

He saved me from my fear, my anguish, my pain, my scars, my life, my death.

He's my commander. He's my lover. He's the only man I have or will ever love with my body, my heart and my soul. I owe everything to Ken Ares.

I don't believe that there is another man on the planet who could have done what he did, no man with the skills or the heart to be what he had to be for me.

When I needed a rescuer, he saved me. When I needed a lover's gaze, he looked at me with so much desire I could never feel ugly again. When I had to be sent home from the war I was trying to fight on my own, he did that. It hurt him to do it, but he did it anyway.

And it still wasn't enough. He came back, wanting nothing more than a sweet little life with me. But when my past came for me, he put aside his desire and became the taskmaster I hated. He became my tormentor. He withstood me looking at him with hate and fear and pain because he knew I had to go through it all to come out the other side.

Now I am his. He owns every part of me. Because there is no chance any part of me would be here if not for him. I love him with every bit of my being, and I will be his in lust, love, and obedience forever.

THE END